Come to the Garden

A NOVEL

JENNIFER WILDER MORGAN

HOWARD BOOKS
AN IMPRINT OF SIMON & SCHUSTER, INC.
New York Nashville London Toronto Sydney New Delhi

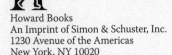

Howard Books
An Imprint of Simon & Schuster, Inc.
1230 Avenue of the Americas
New York, NY 10020

First Howard Books trade paperback edition February 2016

HOWARD and colophon are trademarks of Simon & Schuster, Inc.

For information about special discounts for bulk purchases, please contact Simon & Schuster Special Sales at 1-866-506-1949 or business@simonandschuster.com.

The Simon & Schuster Speakers Bureau can bring authors to your live event. For more information or to book an event contact the Simon & Schuster Speakers Bureau at 1-866-248-3049 or visit our website at www.simonspeakers.com.

Scripture quotations marked (NRSV) are from the New Revised Standard Version Bible, copyright © 1989 the Division of Christian Education of the National Council of the Churches of Christ in the United States of America. Used by permission. All rights reserved.

Scripture quotations marked (NIV) are taken from THE HOLY BIBLE, NEW INTERNATIONAL VERSION®, NIV® Copyright © 1973, 1978, 1984, 2011 by Biblica, Inc.® Used by Permission of Biblica, Inc.® All rights reserved worldwide.

Scripture quotations marked (NLT) are taken from the Holy Bible, New Living Translation, copyright © 1996, 2004, 2007. Used by permission of Tyndale House Publishers Inc., Carol Stream, Illinois 60188. All rights reserved.

Scripture quotations marked (ESV) are from the Holy Bible, English Standard Version, copyright © 2001, 2007 by Crossway Bibles, a division of Good News Publishers. Used by permission. All rights reserved.

Scripture quotations marked (MSG) are taken from *The Message*. Copyright © 1993, 1994, 1995, 1996, 2000, 2001, 2002. Used by permission of NavPress Publishing Group.

Interior design by Jaime Putorti

Manufactured in the United States of America

10 9 8 7 6 5 4 3 2 1

Library of Congress Cataloging-in-Publication Data
Name: Morgan, Jennifer Wilder.
Title: Come to the garden : a novel / Jennifer Wilder Morgan.
Description: First Howard Books trade paperback edition. | Nashville, TN : Howard Books, 2016.
Identifier: LCCN 2015031354
Subjects: LCSH: Angels—Fiction. | Christian fiction. | BISAC: FICTION / Christian / General. | FICTION / Religious. | FICTION / Christian / Classic & Allegory.
Classification: LCC PS3613.O74466 C66 2016 | DDC 813/.6—dc23
LC record available at http://lccn.loc.gov/2015031354

ISBN 978-1-5011-3133-2
ISBN 978-1-5011-3140-0 (ebook)

To my Abba Father God,
who is the delight of my heart

"Stand firm then, with the belt of truth buckled around your waist, with the breastplate of righteousness in place, and with your feet fitted with the readiness that comes from the gospel of peace. In addition to all this, take up the shield of faith, with which you can extinguish all the flaming arrows of the evil one. Take the helmet of salvation and the sword of the Spirit, which is the word of God."

—EPHESIANS 6:14–17 (NIV)

Tilling the Soil:

A NOTE FROM THE AUTHOR

Something mysterious is afoot in my garden—something I want to share.

As a young girl, I loved to listen to the nursery rhyme that contains the phrase "How does your garden grow?" All my life I have been fascinated by the simple beauty of the garden, a sacred space where life is planted, nurtured, harvested, and resurrected.

I have cultivated many gardens in my lifetime. Their roots grow deep and stretch for thousands of miles. My first garden was a tiny flowerpot in the kitchen window of a small apartment in a poverty-stricken neighborhood of Detroit, where I was born and where my father completed his medical residency. Then, in Cleveland, where I was raised, attended school, worked, and married, I took delight in harvesting armfuls of hydrangeas and fragrant lilacs from my spring and summer gardens. And finally, in Houston, where I live now, my backyard gardens are graced with spectacular displays of azalea and gardenia blooms.

All of these treasured gardens have been nurtured by the seasons of life—fertilized by trials and watered with the tears of joys and sorrows. It was here in Houston that I learned how to grow a new and very special kind of garden—a place of hope and healing. It began, of all places, in a hospital room.

In a chance encounter, I was given an opportunity to volunteer in a lay ministry at The Methodist (now Houston Methodist) Hospital in Houston's renowned Medical Center area. This ministry would enable me to put to use hospital skills I had cultivated while living and working in Ohio, along with the compassion born of my faith.

As a lay minister, my responsibility was to visit critically ill patients—to pray with them, to visit with them, and, most important, to *listen* to them. Each time I walked into a patient's room, I created a loving, compassionate, and nonjudgmental space—a safe place that allowed hurting people to share their hearts and stories with me. On the surface, listening appears to be a passive activity, but in reality I found the act of listening to be a powerful force that creates an active exchange. As hearts are unburdened, a space is created for healing and hope to flow back in.

I visited with patients of all faiths, and as they felt permitted to share intimate details of their lives without fear of judgment or ridicule, defenses came down and they talked with me about their encounters with the Divine—their most private, personal confirmations of God's presence in their lives. These emotional testimonies included a full spectrum of encounters: experiencing the awe of God in nature, music, art, literature, and Scripture; angelic interventions and near-death experiences; and encounters with some of the most mysterious of the spiritual gifts, including prophetic visions and the gift of tongues. Week after week, I sat in rapt attention as people told me of angelic bedside visitors, visions of loved ones who had already passed into the heavenly realm, and messages of comfort spoken in dreams in the middle of the night.

This four-year ministry was drenched in redemptive tears, and I was witness to the profound healing that occurs when people are permitted to embrace what they have experienced and to courageously share their stories of encounters with the Divine. One such story moved me so deeply that it literally changed the course of my life.

As I sat next to his bed, "John" told me of his struggle with heart disease that led to an eventual heart transplant. Before his transplant, he experienced several heart attacks, and during his last one, he died. He described in detail how he was carried upward, away from his body in the emergency room, and could see everything occurring as the medical team tried to resuscitate him. He even described the pretty butterfly hair clip that one of the nurses was wearing around her ponytail (which she later confirmed to be true). Then John described being carried up through the ceiling and into a different realm, where he was completely embraced in a warm mist that radiated love in its purest form. As he leaned back to soak in this loving embrace, a voice began to speak. In a very personal conversation, John came to know the Creator, the lover of his soul, whom he had denied and pushed away his entire life. John accepted the love being offered to him and was told he would be sent back to his earthly life.

As he finished his story, John leaned over and looked deeply into my eyes. "Honey," he said, "it is now my life's work to tell others about the incredible love that God offers to each of us, and to encourage them not to wait until the hour of our deaths to accept and share it. We all have important jobs to do for the Kingdom while we live here on earth."

John's powerful testimony convicted me deeply. I, too, have experienced profound encounters with the Divine throughout my life, but I had been fearful of sharing them with others—fearful of being labeled as "one of those." John's courage to share his story finally freed my heart to fully embrace the truth of my own encounters. What a healing moment that was for me!

In a dramatic course-correction that could only have been conceived by God, this quiet little Texas homemaker is now an author. John's story, along with many others, inspired me to offer this freedom and healing to countless others through the pages of this book, by opening the door to my own private garden.

As we near the beginning of my story, there is someone I want to introduce to you. She is as mysterious as the garden you are about to enter. While wrestling with how to write this story, I had a dream, and in my dream I heard the voice of my Lord say very succinctly, "Use an angel!"

I awakened with a start and thought, *What a great idea! But how in the world do I do that . . . I don't know any angels!*

The next morning I snuggled up on the living room couch with my dogs and a steaming cup of coffee, and as I gazed out the tall windows facing the garden, I thought about this possibility of creating an angel to help me. What would he, or she, be like? Would this angel be fierce and warrior-like? A little bit intimidating? Or would it be soft, feminine, and gentle? Would it be a shimmery, invisible kind of figure, or would I be able to see it clearly? Would it talk, or would it just point at things as the Ghost of Christmas Yet to Come did in Charles Dickens's *A Christmas Carol*? Would I be the only one who could see it? Whatever its characteristics were to be, I hoped it would carry with it the wisdom of heaven . . . something I desperately needed in this new venture.

Soon, the character of an intriguing angel named Margaret began to take shape in the eyes of my heart. I would write a fictional story about her, one where she would help me share and make sense of some of the miraculous encounters with the Divine I have had. Some of her attributes admittedly come from my own personality, and the experiences she helps the character Jenn talk through are also my own, but her wisdom . . . well, that belongs exclusively to God.

Margaret brings the wisdom of heaven into my garden, creating a sacred space where I find the freedom to embrace and to share my encounters with God. My story, based in orthodox Christianity, is written for people of all faiths and sentiments, including the absence of faith. We are all spiritual beings on a human journey to find love, acceptance, mercy, mutual respect, and a connection to a Creator.

So, now I invite you to step into my garden, and into this story, with your heart and all of your senses fully engaged. There, among the roses, God's loving presence is revealed to all who are willing to enter.

Truly, *heaven is closer than you think.*

＊ ＊ ＊ ＊ ＊

"I pray that the eyes of your heart may be enlightened in order that you may know the hope to which he has called you, the riches of his glorious inheritance in his holy people."

—THE APOSTLE PAUL, EPHESIANS 1:18 (NIV)

Margaret

Are not all angels spirits in the divine service, sent to serve
for the sake of those who are to inherit salvation?
HEBREWS 1:14

A wispy breath of air played across my face, just enough to tickle my nose and creep across my cheeks. I heard a faraway whisper. It was so faint that I strained to hear, but I just . . . couldn't . . . quite . . . catch up with it.

I awakened with a start. *Did someone just call my name?* Lifting my head, I looked around the room. The Texas sun streamed through the white shutters adorning my bedroom windows, and the house was quiet. I decided it must be my imagination and flopped back down onto my pillow. But I couldn't go back to sleep. Something felt different.

I am not alone.

A tiny knot of concern crept its way into my stomach, and as my other senses fully awakened, I became aware of a strange scent. Eyes closed, I inhaled deeply, trying to place the vague hint of something in the air. *Roses.* It smelled like my favorite white roses.

Where in the world is that coming from? I heard the soft jingle of a dog collar, and this time, I propped myself up on my elbows and looked over to where my whippet, Cody, was nestled in his bed on the floor. His head was up, nose tilted to the ceiling, sniffing the air.

He smells it, too.

Curiosity won over the desire to pull the covers over my head, so I climbed out of bed and slipped into a robe. I paused at the end of the bed to gently tuck blankets over my two smaller pups, who were snuggled together in deep, sweet slumber. A moment of melancholy washed over my heart as I watched them sleep, remembering the sadness of dreams unfulfilled, but Cody's gentle nudge brought me back to the matter at hand. Ears at attention, Cody led the way out of the master bedroom, and together we padded quietly through the house. The smell of roses was much stronger as we entered the kitchen. Nose still in the air, Cody trotted over and sat by the back door while I continued through the house in search of the source of this mysterious scent.

My senses were on full alert as I peeked into closets and peered around doorways. I climbed the staircase to the second floor and searched through bedrooms and office, but found absolutely nothing. As I headed back toward the stairs, I paused in my favorite room in the house—a spacious living area decorated in a safari theme with windows spanning the length of the room. I gazed out the windows overlooking the backyard.

This was my little piece of heaven. Sunlight danced in my gardens, diffused by the leaves of the many giant oak trees gracing our yard. The sparkling, deep-blue waters of the free-form pool undulated gently in the early morning breeze. I sighed. This view never failed to bring peace into the weariest of souls. Suddenly, the air around me was saturated with the fragrance of roses, and then, just as suddenly, the scent disappeared. It was as if the air was gently teasing, pulling me back into this mysterious game of hide-and-seek.

Perplexed, I headed back toward the kitchen, where the scent was most intense. As I entered it, a brilliant flash of light caught my eye, and my attention was drawn to the windows looking out into the backyard. A shimmer of bright blue sparkled once, twice, three times between the stone columns in the garden beside the pool. Edging closer to the window to get a better look, I heard an odd sound. It sounded like laughter—soft, musical laughter. It was coming from everywhere at once, but I still could not see anything. A slight chill ran up my spine, and my skin tingled as if the air was charged with electricity. I began to wish my husband, Guy, had not left for work so early this morning. Cody began to whine and paw frantically at the door.

"What is it, boy? Is something out there?" Cody answered back with a sharp *ruff*. Hesitantly, I opened the door for him and could barely push it all the way open before he bolted outside and disappeared from sight.

At that very moment, a sudden rush of wind blew in through the door. Knocked off balance, I stumbled backward into the kitchen as the door slammed itself shut. The wind softened in its intensity and moved to encircle me. Now I *knew* I was not alone! As I stood embraced in this oddly peaceful, warm whirlwind, the scent of white roses grew stronger. There was an extraordinary gentleness about this wind as it caressed my face, lifted and tossed my hair, and playfully twisted and ruffled my robe and nightgown. And there was something else in the wind—*a presence*. There was a deep sense of invitation in this gentle tempest, as if it were calling my name and ever so delicately encouraging me to step outside. With trembling hands, I opened the door again and slowly walked out onto the back porch, propelled by this strange wind. My heart pounded in anticipation . . . of what?

As I stepped outside, I heard a soft giggle. Turning my head to follow the sound, my gaze fell upon the table and chairs arranged next to the garden. Cody stood there, panting happily as if to say "Look what I found, Mom!" My heart momentarily stopped as I witnessed the source of his excitement. There, standing by the table under the large blue-patterned umbrella, was the loveliest woman I had ever seen.

Her radiant face was framed in a halo of soft, wavy, pure white hair, and her blue eyes twinkled. She was dressed in a cornflower-blue gown that sparkled as if encrusted with thousands of tiny diamonds.

"Good morning, Jennifer," she said. Her smile radiated pure joy. "I'll bet you are surprised to see me."

Surprised didn't even begin to describe what I was feeling. My mouth dropped open, and I stood frozen in midstep. I realized the wind that had carried me outside had disappeared.

"My name is Margaret, dear one, and I am your guardian angel. I have had the blessed privilege of watching over you your entire life."

Somehow, deep down, I knew she was speaking the truth. My mind spun as I tried to comprehend what was happening. *This couldn't be possible . . . could it?*

"W-why . . . y-you're an *angel*? Like, the *heaven* kind of . . . of angel?" I stammered in disbelief.

"That would be me." This angel named Margaret nodded. I could tell she enjoyed this moment immensely.

"What a special day this is," she continued. "Happy birthday to you, Jennifer." With a jolt, I came back to my senses. *My birthday.* I had completely forgotten!

Margaret laughed at my startled expression and said, "Come on over here, dear girl—you need to sit down. You look a bit shell-shocked. Come, sit with me in your beautiful garden." She gathered her gown about her with one hand and sat down in one of the chairs, patting the chair next to her.

Cody scampered away as I crossed over to the table and slid into the empty chair. Margaret was right—my knees did feel a little weak.

"I had completely forgotten about my birthday," I admitted. "I guess I was a little distracted this morning by the house smelling of roses. Thank you for remembering."

"How could I not remember?" Margaret said. "I was here when you celebrated early. It was such a nice party, Jennifer."

As Margaret spoke, I let my gaze wander over the backyard, and my thoughts returned to the recent evening when family and friends had gathered with my husband and me as we'd hosted my dream garden party. On the lawn, tables had been adorned with white linen tablecloths, votive candles, and lovely flower arrangements. And the food! We dined on a scrumptious barbecue feast, including the best bacon-wrapped shrimp this side of the Mississippi. Oh, what wonderful fellowship we shared.

"It was a magical evening, Margaret," I replied, breaking my reverie. "I love birthdays, because life is a privilege worth celebrating. My life has not always been easy, so I cherish these times of celebration with the people I love. God is so good."

"Yes, he is, child," Margaret agreed. Then she reached over and took my hand in hers. "And today heaven is celebrating *you*. Your life, with all of its ups and downs and twists and turns, is an infinite joy to the One who created you. He alone knows the deepest desires of your heart."

Tears began to form in my eyes as Margaret continued.

"That is why I am here this morning, Jennifer. As a special birthday gift to you from your Heavenly Father, I have been sent to fulfill a particularly intriguing desire of yours."

Intriguing desire? Thoughts swirled in my head, my tears instantly forgotten.

Margaret watched me think for a moment and then leaned closer, as if she was about to tell me a secret. In a quiet voice she said, "What if I were to tell you, Jennifer, that what you experience in this world, with your earthly senses, is only a very small part of a much more expansive reality? Does this resonate with you?"

My eyes widened as a stunning realization hit me. I knew exactly what Margaret was referring to. "Oh, Margaret"—I breathed in wonder—"for years I've felt like I have been on the edge of understanding something important, something just outside my grasp. I've had some strange, almost mysterious experiences that I didn't understand, and they raised questions about who I am, what my purpose is, and, most important, whether it is *possible* to connect with the Creator."

Gulp. Now, sitting here under the umbrella with my beautiful visitor, I realized that it is indeed possible. The Divine had just entered my garden!

Margaret laughed, thrilled at my dawning amazement, and I was struck by how unusual and otherworldly her voice sounded, as if accompanied by the sound of tiny chimes.

"Your sense, Jenn, of the importance of these mysterious experiences is more accurate than you realize. You, and others you have encountered, have been experiencing the intersection of the realms of heaven and earth, and I have come to guide you on a journey into the place where these two realms meet. It is in this place that you will discover answers to your deepest questions."

Margaret's confirming words ignited a tiny spark of courage inside me.

"I am so glad you are here to help me with this," I said. "I have been afraid to talk about these mysterious events for fear that people would think I was out of my mind."

"Ah." Margaret nodded, and then asked, "Tell me, child, what exactly is it you have been afraid to talk about?"

The Assignment

All Scripture is inspired by God and is useful for teaching,
for reproof, for correction, and for training in righteousness,
so that everyone who belongs to God may be proficient,
equipped for every good work.

2 TIMOTHY 3:16–17

My lovely angel waited patiently as I willed that spark of courage to stay alive. After taking a slow, calming breath, I began my answer. "I have long believed that God has been speaking to me through mysterious Divine encounters. And, as I guess you already know, I am not alone in this. I have heard stories shared by many others—including family, friends, members of my faith family, and patients I have ministered to. All of us believe that our Creator is speaking to us, and more important that *he wants to be heard.* I think that my deepest questions are *Why is he speaking to us?* and *What does he want us to know?* And, Margaret, there has been an urgent tug on my heart that tells me that the fear of sharing and discussing our encounters with God keeps us from understanding something of crucial importance. That desire you mentioned . . . well, if there are important truths to be learned, I want to discover them and have the courage to share them with others."

Margaret nodded again. Her eyes sparked with an intensity that had not been there a moment before, and I heard something resembling a low rumble of thunder echo in the distance as she began to speak.

"Your desire to overcome your fear and to talk about how God speaks to you *comes from the desire of the Spirit that lives within you to be heard.* The Book of Amos counsels, 'Behold, the days are coming,' declares the Lord God, 'when I will send a famine on the land—not a famine of bread, nor a thirst for water, but of hearing the words of the Lord.' Sadly, this is true for a great many people in the world you live in. Many are not listening, or are afraid to listen for the Creator's voice.

"But you, Jenn, *are* listening. I cannot tell you how much that pleases Our Father! God *is* speaking to you. People all over the world, every day, experience Divine encounters in many different ways. Some recognize the truth of these encounters and give wonderful testimonies, but a great many more do not. Their experiences are discounted as conscience, coincidence, intuition, or imagination. It is imperative, dear child, that all the people of the earth listen to God's voice, because he is the source of life and truth.

"Your own encounters with the realm of heaven have helped you to develop a very personal sense about who God is and how he speaks to you. Would you share a few of your insights with me now?"

I thought for a moment, and then I began to describe some

of my most treasured impressions. "For me, discovering God and hearing his voice was not a thunderous-voice-booming-from-the-clouds event. Instead, God made himself known gently and gradually as I grew up. Then, as I actively began to seek a full-blown relationship with him, I began to experience God on an entirely different level. His presence, and his communication with me, grew in depth and intensity.

"As I have lived my life, particularly during the trials, struggles, and disappointments, God has made his presence known in beautiful, and mysterious, ways. It seems every time God shows up in one of those heavenly intersections, something happens that goes beyond the world's definition of normal. At first, this was frightening and confusing, but eventually, his presence and the way he communicates with me became a part of who I am. Sometimes I am comfortable with that, and sometimes not so much. But I do know this: *There has to be a reason for what God is doing in my life*."

Margaret reached over and gave my hand an encouraging squeeze. "There certainly *is* a reason, my girl!" she exclaimed. "And we will get to that later. Right now I want you tell me a little more about these mysterious ways God speaks to you."

I felt the familiar fear of discussing this subject try to resurface, and this time I ignored it. "One of the most powerful ways God speaks to me is through dream visions, which began in my teenage years. This is difficult to talk about because many people just don't believe this can happen. But I know visions *do* happen. I have experienced them for many years—they are powerful—and I know without question God is speaking to me. For reasons of his own, God decided to communicate with me primarily while I sleep."

I shot a rueful glance at Margaret. "Probably," I said with a sigh, "because my waking mind is far too cluttered with every-day trivialities." Margaret made a noise, something between a snicker and a snort. She obviously knew me pretty well.

"Child," Margaret said fondly, "you are describing what we in heaven call the giftings—the gifts of the Spirit that God provides to help you live the life he has ordained for you. Your dream visions are one of these gifts. God has very specific reasons for the gifts he gives to each of his children. He knows you intimately and he gifts accordingly. And while it may take a lifetime to understand and to use them, be assured that these wonderful and mysterious gifts are living proof that God is truly with you."

The truth in her words sent a delicious shiver through me. Margaret smiled and her intense blue eyes looked deeply into mine. "Your own assurance that your encounters and gifts are real is all you need to begin this journey with me. As for the others you mention who doubt—people will always question what they do not experience or do not understand. That is human nature. All of God's children have the ability to encounter the Divine but must have hearts and minds that are open to the possibility. It is the nature of God to faithfully pursue the human heart, and when one becomes open and vulnerable to him, well, *that*, my girl, is when miracles happen. Anything is possible for one who is willing to believe.

"This brings us to the beginning of our journey, Jenn, and we both have our assignments. I am to guide you in the discovery of the deep and timeless truths God is revealing, and you are to put away your fears and embrace the concept that *heaven is closer than you think*. To do this, you must give yourself permission to approach our journey with the faith of a child—with trust, expectation, and belief.

"Listen, now, and be encouraged by a passage from Scripture that will start us off splendidly. Deuteronomy 29:29 says, 'The secret things belong to the Lord our God, but the things that are revealed belong to us and to our children forever, that we may do all the words of this law.' How wonderful it is that you have the desire to discover and to share with others Divine truths as they are revealed to you! I say we approach this assignment with joy and great anticipation. Are you ready?"

" I . . . think so," I said slowly, "but how do we begin?"

I must have looked like a deer caught in the headlights because Margaret laughed and said, "We will start at the very beginning, of course. *We begin with the faith of a child.*"

Margaret clapped her hands and a loud *crack* filled the air around us, accompanied by that same rumble of distant thunder. A mysterious door had just been flung open, and I knew that our journey had begun.

Fearfully and Wonderfully Made

I have called you by name, you are mine.

ISAIAH 43:1

As the thundering sounds slowly subsided into gentle echoes, Margaret looked over and gave me a bright smile, showing all of her perfect white teeth. It did wonders to calm my pounding heart. Then, without another word, she raised her hands toward the sky and began to recite a portion of one of my favorite psalms.

For you created my inmost being; you knit me together in my mother's womb. I praise you because I am fearfully and wonderfully made; your works are wonderful, I know that full well. My frame was not hidden from you when I was made in the secret place. When I was woven together in the depths of the earth, your eyes saw my unformed body. All the days ordained for me were written in your book before one of them came to be.

As she finished, Margaret said, "You, Jennifer, were fearfully and wonderfully made, for each child is a unique and precious creation of heaven. I think this is a very good place to start—tell me about *your* beginning."

And so I began. "I was born in Detroit, Michigan, in the wee hours of the morning. At the same moment, some two hundred miles away in Anderson, Indiana, my grandmother, whom we called Nana, was awakened in her bedroom by a voice exclaiming, 'Mother!' Nana sat up, startled, because the voice she heard sounded remarkably like my mother calling out to her. She knew immediately that she had to get on a train to make the journey to Detroit. I have often wondered: Was it an angel who spoke to Nana as I was being born?"

I peered over at my new friend, hoping for an answer, but Margaret only nodded for me to continue.

"This strange type of mysterious communication happened at the very beginning of my life, and has occurred throughout my life with startling frequency. My mother has a vivid memory that she has shared with me on more than one occasion. I was not more than five years old, riding in the car with her. Sitting in the backseat, I let out one of my signature squeaky yawns— a yawn accompanied by a not very ladylike sound, like a door opening on creaky old hinges. My mother playfully exclaimed, 'Jennifer! What was that?' I replied very matter-of-factly, 'That was God talking.' If I had only known how prophetic this statement would be."

Margaret burst out in a merry fit of laughter. "Oh, I'm so sorry for interrupting. That just reminded me of how often I heard that funny squeak coming from you at the most inopportune moments while you were growing up. Please keep going."

I chuckled, a little embarrassed at the memory, and continued.

"Even as a very young child, I sensed that somehow God could talk to people, and he was talking to me."

Margaret sighed and said, "It seems like just yesterday you were that sweet little girl with the squeaky yawn. As young as you were, you were just beginning to sense a wonderful truth: *God speaks.* This was the start of a lifetime of learning for you—learning to hear, to listen, to obey, and to discern the truths he reveals in your dreams."

"You're right about the lifetime of learning part, Margaret, because I am *still* learning," I agreed. "I'm afraid I'm not much better than any of my dogs—sometimes I listen and sometimes, well, there are lots of times when it is easier not to listen."

My angel grinned and reached down to pet Cody, who had wandered back over to nuzzle his new friend. He laid his head on her lap and let her scratch behind his ears. I watched with amusement . . . he was the most hardheaded of my dogs, yet I had a feeling he would listen to anything she told him to do.

"Jenn, God will never stop speaking to you, or to any of his children. Even when you are not listening," Margaret said with a knowing smile. "God is a patient and persistent teacher, my dear. And he has instructed me to provide you with personal messages from him along our journey—messages to encourage you and to instruct your heart.

"So, as you reflect upon your earliest days—and that little girl with the squeaky yawn who sensed her Creator's voice—

hear now what God was saying to his fearfully and wonderfully made creation:

"Welcome to your life on earth, my precious little one. I have so much to share with you!"

Thirst

As a deer longs for flowing streams,
so my soul longs for you, O God.
My soul thirsts for God, for the living God.
PSALM 42:1–2

Margaret gave my arm a playful squeeze. "My rather sudden appearance here this morning prevented you from having your morning coffee, Jenn, a treat I know you dearly enjoy. Why don't you go inside and pour yourself a cup? And while you are at it, bring me one, too."

Her eyes sparkled in amusement as she witnessed my astonished reaction. An angel who drinks coffee? I hurried inside and poured two fresh cups of my favorite dark roast. Hannah and Isabel, my other two dogs, followed me back outside. After giving our angelic visitor curious sniffs and friendly tail wags, they wandered off into the yard.

Margaret and I sat together, sipping our coffee and watching the morning backyard activity. Birds hopped from feeder to feeder, and a wary squirrel worked his way down the tree above the birdbath. Comically, he craned his neck to peek around the tree to see where the dogs were roaming in the yard. Confident that their backs were turned, he took his big chance and leapt the rest of the way onto the birdbath, where he took a long drink of water.

We burst into laughter as we watched him finish up and leap back onto the tree, scampering high up into the branches, safe and sound.

"I am amazed, Margaret," I said shaking my head, "at how these creatures have such good instincts. That little squirrel knew he needed water, knew where to find it, and also knew to avoid the danger the three dogs posed to him."

"Where do you think this instinct comes from?" asked Margaret.

"Well, I don't know. I never really thought about it," I mused. "I guess it has just always been there."

"This instinct, Jenn, is lovingly provided to each creature the moment God creates it, so that it will have the knowledge it needs to survive. Humans are given that same gift. An instinct leading them back to the Creator who loves and provides for them. You have sensed this instinct, or this connection, to your Creator in your own life, haven't you?" she asked.

"I have," I replied thoughtfully. "As a young girl, I sensed I came from somewhere else, even though my conscious mind did not remember where. It was a sense of belonging to something special, much larger than me—larger and, at the same time, intensely intimate and loving. I've never completely lost this sense of belonging, though at times in my life I have experienced what I would call momentary breaks, which have caused me great distress."

My angel gave me a knowing look. "My dear, those episodes of distress were telling you that your connection to God is what you need to survive. It is the instinct of the soul to stay connected to its Creator. And when this connection breaks through to the human consciousness, it creates the desire to seek a relationship with God.

"Scripture says *my soul longs for and thirsts for God.* Isn't that a beautiful way to describe this desire to connect with your Creator? In my experience, when people begin to ask the questions 'Who am I?' and 'What is my purpose here?' they are beginning to *thirst,* to sense a connection to something greater than themselves. Do you want to know a secret, dear one?" I nodded as I listened intently to her. "They are beginning to sense their heavenly origin."

Margaret's comment suddenly reminded me of a favorite description of our heavenly beginnings. "I once read a statement that said although we began our existence as citizens of heaven, we have forgotten where we came from, and Jesus came to help us remember and to lead us back.

"I love this description because I really like the idea of being a 'citizen of heaven' first and a citizen of earth second."

Margaret laughed. "Well, as a citizen of heaven, my dear child, I certainly can understand why that would be an appealing thought. You know, young children have some of the best testimonies about their heavenly citizenship, because many retain their memories of heaven for a short time during childhood."

This statement sparked a deep and privately held conviction

of mine that children can and *do* have fleeting memories of an existence that precedes their birth.

"People close to me have shared stories that confirm the very thing you are talking about, Margaret," I said. "A five-year-old boy, an only child, repeatedly asked his parents where his two sisters were, insisting that he already knew them. Additional children were not planned, so imagine their surprise when his parents eventually did have two more children . . . both girls. And then there is the testimony of a three-year-old girl who described to her mother in detail the fluid warmth of her mother's womb and the presence from heaven that kept her comforted and reassured throughout the months leading up to her birth. I wonder, is it possible that guardian angels begin their work while we are being 'knit together in our mother's wombs?'" I shot a questioning look at my angel.

Margaret raised her eyebrows and gave me a mysterious smile but did not answer. In the space of her silence, I took a long, slow sip of coffee and let these last thoughts sink in. It is intriguing to consider our humble existence here on earth is, in fact, only part of a much more expansive existence. Oh, how I wish I could have retained *my* memories of heaven.

"Jennifer," Margaret said quietly, startling me out of my thoughts, "do you see those three sweet little blond heads popping up over the fence in the back of your yard?"

I looked way to the back of the yard, following her gaze, and sure enough, three little blond heads bobbed up and down. I could just barely hear their squeals of delight as these little girls jumped on their backyard trampoline.

Margaret smiled as she watched the children. Their long golden tresses seemed to float in the air with their bouncy, up-and-down motions. Then she whispered, "Even the hairs of your head are all numbered."

I looked over at Margaret, puzzled.

"Dear one," she replied softly, "our Father in heaven loves each of his children so very much. And, yes, he knows you so intimately that he has even counted the hairs on *your* head. Every single person who has walked this earth began their journey in heaven, and each of you has been lovingly and joyfully bounced on our Father's knee. Before he sent you into this world, he whispered something special into your ear, something meant for you and you alone. Even though a veil has been placed over your conscious memory of heaven, your soul remembers God's special whisper. This memory may very well be what you experienced as a young girl when you felt the connection to something intimate and loving."

"I love that," I said, goose bumps forming up and down my arms. "When you put it that way, it sounds as if God began talking to us even *before* we were born."

"Oh, he did indeed." Margaret smiled knowingly. "Listen to what God told the prophet Jeremiah when he called him into service: 'Before I formed you in the womb I knew you, and before you were born I consecrated you; I appointed you a prophet to the nations.'"

Margaret's eyes gleamed as she watched amazement creep across my face as I absorbed these words and the truth behind them.

She continued. "Jennifer, when you sensed that you came from somewhere else, you were correct. During this time of awakening in your young life, your soul continued to hear echoes of God's voice as he called to you from across the veil of the heavenly realm. And this is what he was saying:

"Remember my whisper. You have been mine from the beginning."

Then my angel friend stood and gracefully brushed the folds from her gown. "Let's take a break for a moment. I want to pour myself another cup of coffee, and I will bring one for you, too. While you wait, sit here and let your precious soul reconnect with God's whisper. I'll be right back!"

Heart's Delight

Be still and know that I am God.

PSALM 46:10

Margaret placed our coffees on the table and then wandered over to look at my rose and herb gardens. I remained seated, closed my eyes, and tilted my face to the warm sun, willing my senses to absorb whatever this blessed morning had to offer . . . the trickle of the pool waterfall . . . the occasional cries of glee from the trampolining children . . . the gentle tinkle of wind chimes in the breeze. A blooming sweet almond tree scented the air with its thick perfume. Moments like this are so precious, kind of like a spa moment for the soul.

After several minutes Margaret rejoined me at the table. "Your garden smells wonderful," she exclaimed. "Especially the rosemary."

"Oh, rosemary is one of my favorite herbs," I replied. "It gives me such pleasure to snip it fresh from the garden to add to whatever I'm cooking. And after it rains the fragrance of the rosemary is *heavenly*."

"Mmm." Margaret nodded. "Our Lord gives us such special little gifts every day, gifts for all of the senses." She bent down, picked a sprig of rosemary, and rubbed it between her fingers, releasing its pungent aroma into the air around us.

"This brings me to my next question for you, Jenn. Earlier, you described to me how, as a young child, you sensed the presence of God. Now I want you to tell me how you *experienced* his presence. This is important because your connection to God goes back to the days and experiences of your childhood in ways you may have been completely unaware. You may need to take a few minutes to think about this."

She was right. I sat with my eyes closed and returned to the days of my youth. Despite some hardships, I'd had such a wonderful childhood, with so many varied experiences. How was I going to find the ones Margaret was referring to? Then a thought came to me. When did I experience a quickening in my heart, a stirring in my soul that I could *feel*?

Amazingly, one by one, the memories tumbled in. "Hmmm," I began thoughtfully, "I think the first way I remember experiencing God's presence was while I was being still—a very hard thing for a busy, talkative little girl to be."

Margaret snickered and covered her mouth quickly with her hands, nodding for me to keep going. Okay, I admit, talkative was probably an understatement—and still is!

"As a young girl, I experienced God's presence whenever I felt an unbidden stirring of my heart. For instance, I experienced sensations of *holiness* as I gazed up at the stained glass window in church of Jesus kneeling in prayer. And I felt *timeless* as I lay on the sand and looked up at the night sky filled with stars over Lake Michigan . . . and *wonder*, as I sat in rapt attention listening to a Christmas Eve story about a donkey and other stable animals who knelt at Mary's feet the moment Jesus was born . . . and *calm*, as I put my toes in the water as it lapped softly on the sandy shore of Lake Erie . . . and *contentment*, as I witnessed the love my parents had for each other . . . and *beauty*, as I closed my eyes and immersed myself in the sounds and music of the cello . . . and *love*, as I arrived home from school and was met at the door by the smell of freshly baked chocolate chip cookies . . . and *peace*, as I walked alone on a frigid, moonlit night, snow crunching under my boots and stars twinkling above, bright and clear . . . and *anticipation*, as I awakened on Easter Sunday morning . . . and *delight*, as our caroling group quietly gathered to sing 'Silent Night' at an unsuspecting neighbor's door while candle wax melted all over my mittens . . . and *awe*, as I stood on the shore of the ocean, water stretching as far as the eye could see . . . and *joy*, witnessing a rainbow. Each of these experiences, Margaret, involved the use of one or more of my senses and, for the most part, occurred while I was being *quiet* or *still*."

"You are right, dear one," Margaret affirmed. "The easiest place to find God is in the quiet. It is where you can experience him with all of your senses, since they are not occupied by other things.

"I believe there is another powerful way you have experienced God as a young girl and throughout your life—am I correct?" she hinted.

I nodded slowly and placed my hands over my heart.

"*Music*," I breathed. "Music is and always has been one of the primary ways I experience God's presence. Through the beauty of an orchestra, the words of a hymn, the blend of choral voices, the majesty of a pipe organ . . . the list could go on and on."

Then Margaret asked me something I'd never considered. "Have you ever thought about why and how human beings came up with the idea of music?"

"Well, no, I haven't," I said "But now that you mention it, it seems that from the beginning of time, we have somehow found ways to create lovely, meaningful sounds, *music*, to express our emotions, to celebrate, to mourn."

"Yes, child," Margaret affirmed. "So couldn't it be possible that your souls have already experienced the music of heaven, and as human beings you are constantly trying to re-create what your souls remember—the glorious praise music of heaven's angels?" Her eyes sparkled as she watched my reaction.

Oh, what an intriguing thought! Another reminder of the reality of our heavenly origin.

Margaret positively quivered in her seat, and I knew this was a subject very dear to her own heart. "Music is deeply tied to the human emotions, Jenn, and you became aware of this at an early age on a snowy winter evening. Do you remember?"

"I do," I replied wistfully. "It is one of my most cherished memories. I sat on my daddy's lap by the fire on that snowy winter evening, listening to one of his favorite operas, *La Bohème*. It was early in my childhood. I could not have been more than six years old, and it was the first time I remember hearing opera. It was so intensely beautiful. As Daddy told me the story of Mimi, her love story, and her eventual tragic death from tuberculosis, I vividly remember being filled with so many emotions as the music and story unfolded. Tears streamed down my cheeks as Mimi drew her last breath, and the love of her life cried out for her. My young soul was flooded with feelings way beyond my years, emotions of love and tenderness I did not yet understand, yet they were real. It astounded me I could be so moved by music."

I paused for a moment as I heard a soft sigh. I looked at Margaret, and a small tear was running down her cheek. She remembered this precious evening just as fondly as I did.

"I have read about and heard testimonies from people who claim to have heard exquisite music during near-death experiences. Do you suppose that they were really hearing the music of heaven's angels?" I asked, thinking, *Who better to ask than an angel?*

"Let's see what the scriptures tell us about this," my angel friend answered. "In the second chapter of Luke, shepherds heard the voices of a huge angelic choir singing God's praises the night Christ was born. Can you imagine the awe they experienced on the hillside that night? Then, in the Book of Revelation, the apostle John vividly describes his visions of the music of heaven. In chapter fifteen, verses two to three, he sees believers holding harps and singing, and in chapter five, verse thirteen, he hears all creatures in heaven and earth singing praises to the glory of God.

"Nothing on earth can compare to the music of heaven, but humankind has found beautiful ways to capture the soul's remembrance and apply it to the expression of human emotion. Think about it, dear girl. The sounds of some instruments evoke subdued emotions while others evoke uplifting emotions. Musicians, those who compose and perform, have been gifted with a talent that enables humans to experience the closest approximation to the music of heaven this side of the veil."

"Yes, I understand, Margaret," I replied. "It is like when I listen to the music of the cello . . . there is a mournful beauty about it that stirs my very soul. Sometimes it even makes me weep. It is hard to fathom that music can be even more beautiful than what we experience here on earth."

Margaret rose from her chair, finding it hard to contain her enthusiasm for this subject. "The music of heaven *is* glorious. One day you will hear the music again with heavenly ears—and it will make you want to shout for joy. Oh, what a precious gift our Lord has given his children to carry with them to this world from the realm of heaven!"

Her face radiant, my angel raised her arms and with her ethereal voice she began to sing a psalm of praise.

"Shout for joy to the Lord, all the earth, burst into jubilant song with music; make music to the Lord with the harp, with the harp and the sound of singing!"

Overcome with emotion as she finished, I could only whisper *"Amen."*

Margaret returned to her chair and we sat in silence for several minutes until both of us could get our emotions in check. My thoughts lingered on the joyful words my angel had just sung. She clearly had experienced an act of worship in that moment. Slowly, a new truth began to dawn about the music of praise and why I experience the presence of God when I *sing*.

"You know," I said quietly, "earlier, when you were telling me about the true origin of music, you suggested that our souls remembered the glorious praise music of heaven. I believe, Margaret, that in addition to remembering the music, our souls also remember the *worship* of heaven, and that the actions of praise and worship are intimately and Divinely connected. Something *holy* happens when I sing hymns and anthems at church . . . songs that are filled with the scriptures. It's as if, for a moment, the veil between heaven and earth is lifted and we truly *are* caught up with the host of heaven in the glorious music of praise. In that moment I am no longer just singing . . . I am worshipping, immersed in the presence of God. It is an intensely joyful sensation that I physically can feel."

My angel nodded and looked at me with such tenderness that my eyes began to fill with tears. "Jenn, when we make music . . . when we lift our voices to the Lord . . . a powerful exchange occurs. Our precious voices fill God's heart with joy, and in return, he raises his beautiful voice and covers us with his song of Divine love. Zephaniah chapter three, verse seventeen, tells us that God *rejoices over you with gladness, quiets you with his love, and exults over you with singing.* It is a holy moment indeed when your spirit encounters the song of God! The intense sensation of joy you experience as your Creator sings to you is caused by an anointing of his Divine love. This is a wonderful example of how deep and marvelous your God-given senses truly are. Think back to how you described what you felt upon hearing music, seeing a rainbow, or feeling the snow crunch under your feet. The emotions your senses elicited were love, joy, and peace. These, dear child, are outpourings of the Spirit living within you. Your physical senses activate your spiritual senses, and *that* is how you are able to experience God."

Margaret paused to let this sink in. It was a concept I had never before considered and it was stunning in its simple truth. After a few moments she continued. "Listen now, sweet girl, to what God was singing to you as you experienced his presence with all of your senses during your childhood:

"I am here, dear one, in everything that is beautiful to you. Look for me in all that you love."

Lord, Hear My Prayer

Rejoice in the Lord always; again I will say, Rejoice. Let your gentleness be known to everyone. The Lord is near. Do not worry about anything, but in everything by prayer and supplication with thanksgiving, let your requests be made known to God. And the peace of God, which surpasses all understanding, will guard your hearts and your minds in Christ Jesus.

PHILIPPIANS 4:4–7

My normal morning routine included a fair amount of exercise, and this morning's events had blown "normal" right out the window. Our conversation in the garden had been so riveting, I had not noticed my lack of activity until I shifted in my chair and felt a twinge of stiffness. I rose and moved to the edge of the patio, indulging in a long, luxurious stretch, and oh, it felt good! I looked through my fingertips as they reached toward the sky and marveled at the view. The sky was a pristine, cerulean blue, and the green leaves of the trees glistened with a silver reflection of the brilliant sun.

I had come to think of these trees as my gentle giants, reaching their branches high up into the sky. As a breeze rustled through the treetops, these giants swayed gently back and forth, and I was moved by how they looked as if they were raising their great arms in prayer. Their movements made a whispering sound, like the exhalation of a long, soft sigh. I wondered what prayers or praises they were offering to their Creator. Maybe they were thanking God for another day of life in this beautiful world.

Margaret joined me and matched the direction of her gaze with mine. "Wonderful, isn't it? Even these great trees joyfully communicate with their Maker."

I looked at her sharply. She seemed to know what I had been thinking!

Margaret laughed. "All of creation speaks to God. And you, child, are no exception. As you have just described, you *sensed* God's presence and *experienced* his presence as a young girl. And as I watched you grow up, I was overjoyed to observe you seek God in a new way. You began to *speak* to him."

"I did," I agreed. "It wasn't easy at first, but then I found someone who helped me."

Margaret smiled and held out both hands to me. "Before you tell me about that part of your life, would you join hands with me for a quick prayer?"

I nodded and took her hands in mine. I closed my eyes and waited for her to begin. The breeze swirled playfully around us, and again I detected the faint scent of roses.

In her clear voice, Margaret prayed, "God, come close. Come quickly! Open your ears—it's my voice you're hearing! Treat my prayer as sweet incense rising; my raised hands are my evening prayers."

"Oh, that was beautiful," I exclaimed, touched by these sweet words.

"It *is* beautiful, Jenn. It is the beginning of *The Message's* translation of Psalm one hundred forty one, a prayer written by our beloved King David. I thought it fitting for this next part of your story, which I want to hear about as soon as we sit back down."

I thought to myself, *I wonder if Margaret knows King David? I can only imagine how amazing it would be to sit at his feet and listen to his wonderful prayers.*

As soon as we settled into our chairs, Margaret spoke. "So tell me, Jennifer, about how you began to speak to your Creator. I watched this all unfold, but I want to hear the story from your perspective."

I grinned and began to tell my friend about how I began to speak to God. This was a story I loved to tell.

"I have always been a voracious reader, and one day in my early teens, I stumbled upon a magazine article written by the Reverend Billy Graham about prayer. His article talked about how important prayer is in the lives of God's people, and he said that prayer needs to be an ongoing dialogue between you and God. I was riveted by this statement. Prayer was something I did before going to bed, and my prayers were not very personal or sophisticated. They pretty much consisted of 'Now I lay me down to sleep' with a few thank-yous and blessings mixed in. And, admittedly, many nights I just plain forgot to say my prayers.

"As I read, I thought to myself: *An ongoing dialogue? Would God listen to me if I talked to him during the day?"*

I paused for a moment and gazed at Margaret. She was nodding her head, trying very hard not to say a word.

"Reverend Graham's article really bothered me because I felt that maybe God wanted me to be communicating with him more, and I was not doing what he wanted. And I could not pray in the beautiful prayer language our minister used in church. My prayers sounded childlike compared to his. How could I talk with God, the Creator of the universe, the great I AM, without being able to use the grown-up, flowery language of prayer I was used to hearing? After contemplating this for a day or so, I got out pen and paper and proceeded to write a letter to Reverend Graham.

"My letter was very straightforward. I asked Reverend Graham how to pray so that God would listen to me. I mailed my letter with a great sense of anticipation, and then I waited . . . and waited.

"Time passed, and I completely forgot about my letter. My teenage girl mind was otherwise occupied by boys and the music heartthrobs David Cassidy, Donny Osmond, and Bobby Sherman. Then one day my mother entered my bedroom with a rather amazed look on her face. She held up an envelope and said, 'Jennifer, you have a letter from Billy Graham!'

"Wow! I did indeed have a response from Reverend Graham. He thanked me for my letter and for my thoughtful question. In his response he explained that prayer was something everyone could do, children and adults alike. 'All you have to do,' he wrote, 'is to talk to God like he is your friend. Just tell him whatever is in your heart. Don't worry about using fancy words. He loves you and wants to hear from you.' I asked myself, *Could it really be that simple?*

"It took some practice, mostly to *remember* to pray, but I began that very day talking to God as if he were my friend. And I discovered that Reverend Graham's advice really *was* simple. I gave God thanks for the things I had, the people I loved, and asked him for help with the problems I had—some silly school stuff, and some not so silly stuff.

"When I was fourteen, my grandfather, a physician, noticed a lump in my neck and talked to my father, also a physician, about it. I ended up seeing a surgeon who recommended surgery because it might be cancer. My mother had recently lost her best friend to breast cancer, so the word 'cancer' and the thought of possibly having it scared the living daylights out of me. I was so glad to be able to talk to God about it, and I did, a lot. The night before I had to go to the hospital, I lay in my pretty little twin bed and prayed. I was really scared, and yet a wonderful peace came over me while I prayed. It felt as if someone had their arms around me, and I knew I would be okay, no matter what the outcome was. I was actually able to go to sleep that night. The surgery went on as scheduled, and doctors successfully removed a benign growth from my thyroid gland. No cancer.

"What helped me the most was being able to talk to God through the whole process, and I began to have an assurance that he was listening. I owe my heartfelt thanks to Reverend Graham for taking the time to answer a young girl's question. It made a monumental difference in my life."

Margaret sat very still for a moment and then looked at me, her blue eyes misting with tears. "It did make a monumental difference, Jennifer, because once you learned how to pray with the assurance that God was listening to *you*, you were ready to learn *two-way* communication with the Almighty—to learn how to listen to *him*. You were very fortunate indeed to have had the guidance of Billy Graham. He has used his anointing well and has prayerfully led millions of souls to the throne of our precious Lord. And, child, no one knows better than our Lord the value of prayer. While Jesus was here on earth, he relied on prayer to keep in constant touch with his Heavenly Father.

"So, my dear girl, as you began to talk to our Father in heaven with heartfelt innocence and expectation, he was whispering back to you. Listen closely . . . he has never stopped whispering this prayer:

"I love to hear from you, my beloved child. I am always listening, hoping to hear your sweet voice. From your lips to my heart."

A wistful sigh escaped Margaret's lips as she continued. "How I wish all of God's children knew how dearly he wants to hear from them each day. His heart longs to hear from his beloved, no matter what time of the day or night."

Margaret smiled at me, and as she did, I began to detect the scent of white roses in the air again.

"I am going to leave you for a while and let you get on with your day. After all, it is your birthday. Go celebrate with your friends. I expect you will have lots to tell them." She winked knowingly.

Disappointment seeped into my heart.

Margaret sensed my disappointment and gave me an amused look. "Oh my, don't worry, Jenn. I am not nearly through with you yet. We have much, much more to discuss. Have a wonderful day, and I will return here at sunset. Will you meet me out here then?"

"Of course I will," I replied.

"Until tonight, then." She blew me a kiss and walked out into the backyard, her gown shimmering until she disappeared into thin air.

I stood and stared for a moment at the space Margaret had just occupied, missing her already. I have always longed for the hours of my birthday to stretch out endlessly, wanting to savor every moment. But today I could hardly wait for nightfall.

Ask, Seek, Knock

And I tell you, ask and it will be given to you; seek, and you
will find; knock, and it will be opened to you. For everyone
who asks receives, and the one who seeks finds, and to the
one who knocks it will be opened.

LUKE 11:9–10

I headed excitedly toward the cozy corner table in my favorite
Italian restaurant, where my two dearest friends, Linney and
Grace, waited. It wouldn't feel like my birthday if I didn't celebrate with them. As I approached, I was greeted with big hugs
and happy birthday wishes.

"You are glowing, Jenn," said Grace.

"Yeah," agreed Linney, "you must have received something
pretty special for your birthday."

"You don't know the half of it," I replied. "Sit down, girls, because I have something extraordinary to share with you."

After ordering our lunch, Linney and Grace leaned forward,
eager to hear what I was so excited about. As I told them about
waking up to the scent of roses and discovering an angel named
Margaret in my garden, I observed two very different reactions.

Grace's eyes got bigger and bigger as she listened, and a huge smile spread across her face. She soaked in every word. But Linney sat quietly, her big blue eyes puddled with tears. My heart sank, because I got the feeling she didn't quite believe me . . . maybe she was even feeling a little sorry for me . . . or, maybe for herself. That familiar fear of sharing rose up inside me again. I really did not want one of my dearest friends to think I was "one of those" . . . someone who got carried away with an overactive imagination—someone who believed in things unseen.

As I finished my story, Grace talked nonstop about how wonderful this birthday gift was from God. Finally, Linney reached over, took my hand, and spoke, interrupting Grace. "Jenn, I can see that you really believe what you experienced is real. I just don't know what to think. I've never experienced anything like this, and I need a little time to process what you just told us. I really *want* to believe you, but an angel in your garden? *Really?*" She sighed, gave my hand a gentle squeeze, and continued. "I'll tell you what. I'm just going to be happy for you, because I love you."

Her sweet words made me smile. Her friendship, and Grace's, meant the world to me. I privately wondered which reaction I would encounter more frequently in the future if I continued to share my Divine encounters with others. I suspected it might be more like Linney's. Margaret was right, I acknowledged quietly to myself. *This desire I have to tell others about my experiences is going to take a lot of courage.*

Grace's chatter brought me out of my thoughts as she asked, "Do you think we could come over and meet Margaret?"

Her question gave me pause. I had no idea if they would be able to see and talk with Margaret as I did. I said that I would leave it up to Margaret.

Soon our conversation turned to our husbands, and I felt slightly guilty I had not yet been able to tell Guy about my amazing visitation. I hoped with all my heart that he would at least be receptive. As the afternoon hours began to slip toward evening, the three of us reluctantly parted with many hugs and promises to reconvene often for lunch and to speak of miracles—or at least the *possibility* of miracles.

A trio of happy pups enthusiastically greeted me at the door as I got home. Their love was such a gift in my life. It is no wonder to me that the word *dog* is *God* spelled backward. I puttered in the kitchen for a while and set out some food to thaw for dinner—it would be a late meal as Guy had an end-of-day meeting that could not be rearranged.

Finally, I began to count the minutes until the arrival of sunset, when my angel was to return. At the appointed hour, I stepped out onto the patio. No Margaret, yet. The evening air was still quite warm, so I sat down at the pool's edge and dangled my bare legs in the cool water. Slowly moving my legs back and forth, creating big swirls in the water, I thought about my morning conversations with Margaret. As my wise angel friend had led me systematically through the ways I experienced God during the various stages of my young life, it had become evident that he had been a consistent part of my life since before I was born. What a delicious truth! I began to see reflections of orange and pink in the swirls of blue water, and I lifted my face to the sky.

Tonight's sunset was breathtaking. Huge streaks of brilliant, fiery orange and pink raced across the sky as if they had been finger painted on a vast canvas with a giant hand. The lovely view brought to mind a saying I had heard somewhere before: "The sunrise is God's greeting, and the sunset is his signature." I closed my eyes and whispered a prayer of thanks for such a beautiful signature to the end of a very special birthday.

A sudden movement in the air next to me caused my eyes to snap open. There was Margaret, sitting next to me, dangling her legs in the water next to mine!

"Did you enjoy your time with your friends today?" Margaret asked.

I nodded, my heart thrilled at her return. I told her about my conversation with Linney and Grace, and of their different reactions.

"You were right, Margaret," I said. "Some people have a very hard time believing what they have not experienced for themselves . . . or believing in something they cannot see. That made me wonder . . . would my friends be able to see you?"

Margaret shook her head. "No, child, they would not. You, and your sweet pups, are the only ones who can see me. This journey of discovery we are on was designed for your eyes and ears only, because it is *your* story. And, once you begin to share your story, you will open the eyes and ears of many others. I assure you, those who seek the truth *will* find it," she added with a knowing smile.

We sat together, watching the colors of the sky deepen, adding hues of lavender and purple. The soft swirls of water reflected pink, orange, blue, lavender, and purple, mixing gently like an artist's watercolor palette.

"A beautiful sunset, isn't it, Jenn?" Margaret asked.

"I couldn't think of a more perfect ending to today," I agreed with a quiet sigh. "God truly has had his hand on this day, from beginning to end. It began with a house filled with the scent of white roses, then your miraculous appearance, and now it ends with this gorgeous sunset."

"Mm . . . " Margaret replied, nodding in blissful agreement. She leaned down, scooped up some water, and let it trickle back into the pool through her fingers. I watched as her whole body began to shimmer and glow with a soft light. The large drops falling from her fingers formed ever-expanding rings in the water, which also began to shimmer with this mysterious luminescence.

Margaret looked at me and said tenderly, "Tonight's sunset carries with it the promise of a new sunrise—a new beginning." She reached over and cupped my face in her hands, the luminescent water wetting my cheeks as it dripped from her fingers. Then she said softly, "Jesus said, 'Those who drink the water I give will never be thirsty again. It becomes a fresh, bubbling spring within them, giving them eternal life.'

"I was a witness, dear child, to a new beginning for you as you made the most important decision of your young life and jumped heart first into the waters of eternal life. Our Heavenly Prince remembers so fondly the moment you opened your heart and your life to him and the joy it brought to all of us in heaven. He would like for you to share that story with me now."

I felt a thrill of excitement run up and down my spine. I couldn't think of a better ending to this precious day than to tell my angel friend about the events leading to that day long ago when my heart was changed forever.

"When I was in the eighth grade, my family attended the beautiful Old Stone Church in Cleveland, Ohio. That year I enrolled in communicants' class. This class prepared young people to officially join the church, declare Christ as Savior, and receive communion at a ceremony held on Maundy Thursday. Our minister was a fiery redhead—a former Canadian fisherman, if my memory serves me correctly—and oh, could he preach! He had a deep love for the Lord, and you could feel his passion in his sermons. I often sat listening to him and thought it would be so nice to have such a passion for God, but it just was not there for me yet. Pleasant and lovely feelings, yes, but *passion*? No.

"I completed my communicant's curriculum with my fellow classmates and was formally initiated into the church. I still have the little white Bible presented to me by a dear family friend on that special day. Being able to take Communion with my parents and all of the adult church members from that day forward was a great privilege. But something still seemed to be missing. I wasn't feeling the passion I had expected. When I heard people speak of their personal relationships with Christ, I kind of scratched my head. Huh? *Personal* relationship? I just didn't get it."

At this, a very unangel-like snort erupted beside me. I looked over to see Margaret again with both hands pressed firmly over her mouth, lest she dare let out any more sounds.

Her eyes were squinched tightly shut and her shoulders bobbed up and down.

Good grief. I sighed to myself. She obviously knew me pretty well—there are lots of times I just don't get it. My husband derives much amusement in hearing me say "I don't get it!" after a joke he has just told.

"Hey, Margaret," I said to her, "a little support here, please. I am getting to the part where I finally got it!"

"So sorry," she said in a quivering voice, obviously still trying to rein in her glee. "Please continue."

"Okay. Let's fast-forward to the summer of 1974, when my family traveled to our annual vacation destination in Traverse City, Michigan. My father shut down his busy medical practice for two weeks, and he and my mother packed our family and supplies into the station wagon and made the eight-hour drive to our log cabin on the bay of Lake Michigan. Oh, how we all loved it there! Sandy beaches, pine forests, beautiful, cold, clear water, a raft to swim out to . . . and our cousins. My aunt Adrienne and uncle Don and their family traveled to Traverse City from Indiana every year at the same time for a three-week stay. It was such fun to have this time to be together. This particular year, things were a little different. As our two weeks came to a close, one of my older teenage cousins wanted to go home with my family to take in some Cleveland Indians baseball games, and I wanted to stay an extra week at the beach. So we worked out a trade. My cousin would go to Cleveland, and I would stay with Adrienne and Don and family for an extra week, and then we would make a kid exchange somewhere in between Ohio and Indiana.

"My aunt and uncle were accomplished sailors and had their red-and-white sailboat with them. Every day during that extra week, they took me sailing out on the bay. I remember being very afraid of the deep, blue water, knowing it was way over my head. Uncle Don, formerly an engineer, had responded to God's calling in his life and had become pastor of an Indiana church. While we sailed, he told me a story from the Bible about when Jesus was in the boat with his disciples, who were also afraid. He told me about how Jesus calmed them and calmed the storm. I learned a lot about Jesus in the days that followed. I felt my heart changing, kind of like how in Dr. Seuss's *How the Grinch Stole Christmas*, the Grinch's heart grew three sizes bigger in one day! My little white Bible was filling up with notes and underlined scriptures. I could not get enough of this wonderful Jesus, who, really, if it could be possible, wanted to be my *friend*. I quite literally was falling in love with him. By the end of the week, I asked how I could go about receiving Jesus as my personal Savior, since I took seriously his promise in Luke chapter eleven, verses nine to ten. With great joy, my aunt and uncle knelt with me at my bedside in prayer, and I prayed six simple words: *'Jesus, please come into my life.'*

"Guess what, Margaret," I said, "I finally *got* it!"

She beamed at me. "You sure did. And you should have seen the celebration in heaven when you spoke those precious words. *'For there is joy before the angels of God over one sinner who repents.'*"

Just the thought of angels rejoicing for little ol' me made my heart leap. I enjoyed the image for a minute, and then I continued with my story.

"The first thing that happened after I spoke those six words was that I saw another word form in my mind. It was *kham*. I was puzzled and asked my aunt and uncle what it meant. They answered simply, 'Just say it.' So I said it, and oh my goodness! Words of a language unknown to me came pouring forth from my mouth. It went on and on, and the most incredible joy was bubbling up inside me so fast I couldn't hold it inside anymore. I burst out laughing, and my aunt and uncle did, too. I believe, Margaret, that this was one of the giftings you mentioned earlier—my first gift of the Spirit. It was completely unexpected, and a bit puzzling, since I could not understand any of the words."

"Let me interject something here," interrupted Margaret. "This gift of the Spirit God gave you is quite real, and I know you have come across people in your life who have made you feel uncomfortable about it. I will ask you more about this later on. But, for now, I want to hear the rest of your story."

I continued. "When I returned home to my family, I needed some time to come down from my 'mountaintop experience'— to get my elation and exuberance for the Lord to a manageable state. I think I drove everyone a little crazy for a bit. But I finally settled down and got busy with school and all the things that go along with being a flaky teenage girl. There was something different about me, though. Because now I knew in my heart that Jesus was my friend and, no matter what I was feeling, I could talk to him. For me, that was huge. I particularly recall one day in dance class: I was auditioning for a dance team and had to successfully complete several required moves that did not come easily to me. Much to my chagrin, I was not the most graceful dancer."

I shot Margaret a look before she could break into laughter. "No comments, please, from the peanut gallery. I am freely admitting my klutziness." She just nodded and pressed her lips together tightly to suppress what I had rightly suspected was going to erupt.

"When it was my turn to perform a dance step across a balance beam, I knew I was in big trouble. I was about to be evaluated for grace and balance, and I'd never been able to do this in practice without falling off the beam. So, I breathed a quick prayer asking Jesus to help me with this. I stepped onto the beam and began dance-stepping across. Then the most amazing thing happened. I felt someone holding my hand! *Really, truly, holding my hand.* I danced across the beam flawlessly! I know that something really special happened that day. And I made the dance team—as an apprentice—but I made it.

"This was an important time of awakening in my life. I knew that with all of my flaws, God loved me and was truly there for me. I was gaining assurance that when I prayed, he was listening. I began to have confidence in my relationship with the Almighty, and my heart was filled with love for him. The passion I had longed for was finally inside of me."

Margaret's eyes were filled with happy tears as I finished my story. "Yes, you did find your passion, and you could finally take the words of Deuteronomy chapter six, verse five, into your heart and live them: 'You shall love the Lord your God with all your heart and with all your soul and with all your might.'"

Then Margaret leaned in close and spoke in a conspiratorial whisper, "You were right about something special happening on that dance beam. At the request of our beloved Jesus, *I was the one holding your hand.*"

I thrilled at this revelation. Both Jesus and Margaret had been there on that day long ago when a young high school girl so badly wanted the chance to fit in.

Margaret dipped her hands in the water once more and took both of my hands in hers. "Precious child, when you knelt at that bedside and jumped head and heart first into the waters of the promise of eternal life, Jesus rejoiced. And this is what he said to you as his heart was bursting with joy:

"I am yours forever, my beloved, for you are now baptized in me. I can't wait to explore our future together."

"Now, Jennifer, we are about to go much deeper into our journey." Margaret said, her voice taking on a more serious tone. "Your relationship with Jesus ushered you into a new future— a future where you began to encounter the things unseen."

Dream Girl

I slept, but my heart was awake.

SONG OF SOLOMON 5:2

The next morning dawned warm and humid. With a tender kiss I handed my groggy and bewildered husband his briefcase and watched him walk out the back door. He stopped by the edge of the pool and looked over toward the chairs and table arranged by the garden. A shake of his head and a sudden, bright smile indicated his recollection of last night's extraordinary conversation. Following an intimate candlelit birthday dinner on the porch, I told Guy the same story I had shared earlier in the day with Linney and Grace. I watched his face closely as I told him about my angelic backyard discovery. He listened quietly and intently, and then a small smile began to play at the corners of his mouth, as if a new realization was dawning as I spoke.

"Well, what do you think?" I asked, as I finished my story. "Do you believe me?"

Guy leaned back in his chair and looked past me into the night—the garden was quiet, asleep. Finally, he looked at me and said, "To answer you, Jenn, I want to tell you a story. Do you remember when I went deep sea fishing with a client of mine several months ago?"

I nodded.

"Well," he continued, "I stood on that boat, a hundred miles out in the Gulf of Mexico, with my fishing line in the water. As the waves slowly moved across my line and splashed against the side of the boat, I watched in frustration as the men all around me were pulling in big fish, but I did not even have a bite. Finally, I reeled in my line and noticed the bait was gone. I guessed it had fallen off, so I re-baited and put my line in again. But, still no bites . . . only the wave action hitting my line and splashing the boat. I was about to give up and then I had a thought. Maybe the slight pull on the line I felt every time the wave hit it was really a fish nibbling on my bait. So the next time I felt the tug of the wave move across my line, I yanked upward and, to my surprise, I had hooked something . . . a huge red snapper. I tried the same thing again, and, bingo! Another snapper. Up until this point, I had been completely oblivious to what was really going on deep beneath the water's surface—what I thought was wave action was really a bite. I just did not recognize it for what it really was."

Guy paused for a moment, just as I was beginning to wonder where in the world he was going with this story. But then he continued.

"As I listened to you tell me about your angel, I felt several strange tugs on my heart, encouraging me to believe. I was suddenly reminded of that wave action tugging on my fishing line.

I think that feeling is similar to what we experience when God is trying to make himself known to us. Beneath the surface of our daily lives, from an unseen place, he is constantly tugging at our consciousness. We just have to recognize those tugs for what they really are . . . demonstrations of his presence. And you, Jenn, seem to be able to do that. So, yes, I do believe you have had a Divine encounter. I believe God is making himself known to you through this angel named Margaret—she is teaching you to recognize his presence."

Wow. That was quite a conversation.

Now, as I watched Guy stand, marveling, in the morning garden where Margaret and I met, I whispered a prayer of thanks for my insightful husband who had a heart open to possibility, and to the presence of God.

After he pulled out of the driveway, I turned my attention to the chores at hand, picking up dog toys and washing a few dessert dishes left in the sink. Mostly, I tried to keep my eyes off the clock, for I was eagerly awaiting Margaret's return. She had left me just after sunset the night before and had promised an early morning appearance. Suddenly, as I passed by the kitchen window with a large load of laundry in my arms, I again saw a shimmer of light in the garden. I hurried into the laundry room, threw the pile on the floor, and ran outside, holding my breath and pleading silently, *Please, oh, please, let that be my Margaret!*

Sure enough, I found her standing beside the pool where we had sat last evening, a vision of loveliness. Today her sparkling gown was a pale buttercup yellow. "Good morning to you, Jennifer." She beamed, her smile reflecting the light of heaven.

I practically ran over to join her. I was astounded at how much I loved this angel I had just met.

We stood together on the patio, watching God's creatures celebrate the beginning of the new day. Birds, butterflies, and squirrels flitted and jumped and played among the trees and flower beds. Margaret spied my statue of St. Francis of Assisi in one of my garden beds. She strolled over to get a closer look, and I followed.

"This is a nice choice for your backyard, Jennifer. Did you know that Francis called the birds and animals of the earth his brothers and sisters?"

"Yes, as a matter of fact, that is one of the reasons I have always felt so close to Francis, because birds and animals are so close to my own heart. St. Francis has popped up in my life so many times in art, literature, and nature that I just had to put him in my garden."

Margaret continued on, walking deeper into the yard, and as she stepped from the shadows of the trees into the sunlight, the most remarkable sight met my eyes. I saw the faintest glimmer behind her shoulders. Was it . . . I did a double-take and squinted hard, trying to make out what I was seeing. Again, a glimmer, a shimmer . . . an outline of *wings*. Huge, head-to-toe, *beautiful, transparent wings*!

"Margaret!" I exclaimed. "I didn't know you had wings. They're beautiful! Have you had those all along?"

"Why, yes," she replied. "I just chose this time to reveal them to you. And I did it to show you something. Just as you were not able to see my wings until I stepped into the light, your eyes and heart did not see God's deeper truths until he chose a time to reveal them to you. As I move back into the shadows, you will no longer see my wings, but they are still there. God's truth is also always there. It was there at the very beginning and will be there for eternity. To see it, all we need to do is look into the Light—the Light of the World."

I nodded and blinked back tears. I had nothing coherent to say at that moment.

She smiled in understanding, and her blue eyes crinkled up at the edges.

"We have come to the stage in your life when new and important gifts are emerging, and I would like to start with your dreams. Can you tell me, Jenn, what began to happen while you slept?"

A small frown planted itself on my face as that familiar fear rose up inside me. Noticing, Margaret put her arm around my shoulders and began to steer me back to our table. "Walk with me, child," she said tenderly, "and listen to these words from Scripture, for they may encourage your heart: The second chapter of Daniel, verse twenty-eight, says, 'There is a God in heaven who reveals mysteries . . . Your dream and the visions of your head as you lay in bed are these.' And in Jeremiah chapter thirty-three, verse three, the Lord tells Jeremiah, 'Call to me and I will answer you, and will tell you great and hidden things that you have not known.'"

As we headed back to the table together, I admit I was still preoccupied by the revelation of Margaret's wings. But the scriptures Margaret quoted were so strikingly appropriate to my own life's experience that, by the time we settled comfortably in our chairs, I had regained my courage. I began to answer Margaret's question.

"Shortly after I began my personal relationship with Christ, I began to dream. Not just any dreams, but dreams that left me with feelings of concern, amazement, and, quite honestly, a healthy dose of fear. But they all had one common denominator— I was being given information about current or future events that no one else knew. These dreams started out about things of this world and everyday life, and later moved to include deep, sacred, or spiritual, truths."

I hesitated. This is a subject I rarely spoke openly about.

"Keep going, Jenn," Margaret prompted. "Tell me about your earliest dreams."

"The first dream I had was about my grandmother. I dreamed she was walking out of an office building and descending a set of stairs. Halfway down the stairs, she tripped and fell, rolled down the remaining steps, and landed at the bottom, her back broken. When I awakened, I was so relieved to realize that this had only been a dream.

"However, my relief did not last long. I cannot recall the time of year this was, but I do remember that my family was sitting down in the dining room having breakfast together later that morning, so it must have been a weekend or holiday. The telephone rang while we were eating, and my mother got up from the table to answer it. She came back a little while later with a stricken look on her face. She said, 'Nana fell and broke her back.'"

"Sitting in my seat, I felt the floor rushing up to meet me and ringing in my ears. I was so shocked I nearly fainted. I wondered if I had caused this because I'd dreamed it. As it turned out, she did not fall exactly as I saw it in my dream—she fell at home. But the fact remained—I knew it before anyone else did. I don't believe I mentioned this to anyone because I was terrified. Thankfully, Nana recovered and my dreams returned to their normal harmless wackiness. What was very unsettling to me, though, was that *my prayers to Jesus about this incident were met with silence.*"

I hesitated again, looking to Margaret for some possible insight. Instead, she reached over and gave my arm a little squeeze. "That was indeed an unsettling experience for you," she affirmed. "You're doing fine . . . keep going."

Obeying her prompt, I continued. "The summer I turned twenty, I had the opportunity to go to England and Scotland as a chaperone for a high school marching band. The school was my alma mater, and my sister marched with the band as a flag carrier. The band was making a trip from Cleveland, Ohio, to the town of Redcar, in Cleveland County, England. My father was accompanying the band as the attending physician, and my mother as another chaperone. We were all so excited as the date for our departure in June approached. As excited as I was, I was also experiencing a strange and unusual dread. I had numerous dreams of problems with the airplane on our trip. I loved to fly and had never experienced problems on a flight. I chalked it up to nerves and excitement, but as the date drew closer, my dread increased to the point I almost told my parents that I did not want to go on the trip. After telling myself a thousand times that I was just being silly, the date arrived. We went to the airport and boarded our plane from Cleveland to Boston. The flight went off without a hitch. We arrived in Boston and went to the gate to board our next plane, which would take us across the Atlantic to Glasgow, Scotland. When we got to the gate, I could hardly believe my eyes. There in the window was the giant nose of the biggest plane I had ever seen! It was a Boeing 747.

"The plane loaded, doors closed, and we were off. There were two aisles and three sections of seats—one on each side and one in the middle. I sat in the middle section ahead of the wings next to my father. On the other side of me sat a rather obnoxious teenage boy who was a drummer with the marching band and, to my chagrin, kept playing imaginary drums on his tray table. Not fifteen minutes into the flight, there was a large *bang* and the plane veered on its right side, then veered on its left side, then straightened out. 'Cool!' exclaimed drummer boy next to me. *Not cool*, I thought. I had flown enough to know this was not normal. A minute later, a flight attendant approached my father and quietly requested his presence in the back of the plane. He got up and went with her. Then the pilot's voice came over the loudspeaker: 'Ladies and gentlemen, we have experienced a problem, and one of our four engines is damaged. The engine caught fire, and the fire has been extinguished. We could make it across the ocean with the remaining three engines, but for safety's sake, we have decided to return to Boston. The problem is that we have a full fuel tank and we are too heavy to land, so we're going to have to circle and dump fuel until we are light enough to turn around and land back in Boston." My father came back and told us that a woman in the back had become hysterical because she was sitting behind the wing and saw the engine catch fire. *Great.* My thoughts quickly returned to the feelings of dread and the dreams of problems with the airplane I had been experiencing during the prior months. What was God trying to tell me? Had he really wanted me to cancel my flight? Or, as I was beginning to suspect, was there another message hidden in all this?

"It took about twenty minutes of circling and dumping fuel before we could attempt a landing in Boston. I felt so helpless in the air for those twenty minutes, knowing there was a serious problem with the plane, and I said a lot of prayers. As the plane neared the airport, we could see fire trucks lining both sides of the runway. Our landing was uneventful—no more fire. The airline did not have another plane available in Boston for us, so they had to have another 747 flown in from LaGuardia Airport in New York City. In the meantime, they would not let us exit the damaged plane, so they served us a meal while we waited. I remember feeling desperate to get off that plane. As soon as the new 747 arrived and we had boarded it, the dread I had been feeling for so long instantly vanished. I knew this next flight would be a breeze, and it was. An interesting sidenote to this story is that my mother had also been having the same dread and reservations about flying on this trip, and neither of us had voiced our feelings."

As I finished telling Margaret this story, I confided to her that this experience caused me to consider there was a lot more going on than just dreaming. At least for me.

Margaret nodded in agreement. "You are correct, Jennifer," she said. "God was not trying to frighten you or confuse you with these strange new experiences. Instead, he was teaching you to begin to pay attention to your dreams. And you were a good student, because that is exactly what happened." She smiled and continued. "Now, I want you to tell me the dream you had about the baby."

The baby. This dream had *convinced* me that another realm was pushing its way into my consciousness while I slept.

"In the mid-1980s, I was living in Cleveland, Ohio. Friends of mine, whom I had not seen in several years, were expecting their first child. During the eighth month of my friend's pregnancy, I dreamed there was a serious problem with the baby's heart, and that the baby might die. It was a very disturbing dream, and kind of strange because I had not been in touch with her recently. I wondered why on earth I would be dreaming about her baby. My previous experiences with dreams coming true made me think twice about this one. What was I supposed to do? Call a very pregnant friend I had not seen in a long time and tell her something was wrong with her baby? I think not! Again, I let this go, telling myself that for the most part, my dreams are just dreams and do not come true.

"The baby's due date finally arrived, and my friends were blessed with a baby boy. But immediately, things went terribly wrong. He turned blue. He was rushed to the neonatal intensive care unit, where it was determined that he was born with a condition called transposition of the great vessels, meaning that the two major vessels of the heart were reversed. The baby would die without immediate open-heart surgery to correct the problem. He was taken to another hospital with a pediatric heart specialist and underwent an open-heart procedure. Thankfully, the procedure was a success and this dear little boy survived."

I paused and looked over at Margaret, who was listening intently. I sighed. "You know, Margaret, by this time, I was convinced God had some kind of purpose for showing me these things in my dreams. But for the life of me, I could not figure out what this purpose was. It both frightened and amazed me. I knew I could not have called my friend and told her what I had dreamed. It would have scared her to death, and she probably would have thought I had lost my mind. But I also was getting the clear impression that *this dreaming was not to be ignored.*"

Margaret stood and moved slowly around the table to stand behind me. She placed both of her hands gently on my shoulders. In a hushed voice she said, "You were correct in your impression that you were not to ignore these special dreams.

"I want you to do something now. Close your eyes and picture this in your mind: Dreaming is like resting up against a heavy wooden door with huge iron hinges. Feel it. The door is solid, immoveable, secure. Just like your childhood dreams, it is just there. It may lead somewhere, but you are not particularly interested in where. You are only interested in waking up after a pleasant rest.

"Then, as a young woman, your dreams change. They take on meaning. They come true. They cause you angst. You know there is a purpose, but you don't know what it is. You are curious and are now pressing your hands against the door. Suddenly you hear the sound of huge tumblers falling into place as a great lock becomes unlatched. The hinges creak mightily, and the door cracks open barely an inch with a tremendous shudder. You peek inside, trying to get a glimpse of what is beyond. There is a light approaching . . . you press harder . . .

"Now, Jennifer!" Margaret commanded, flinging her arms wide. "Throw open this door and feel the light of God's truth as it comes flooding out upon you. What do you think God was telling you by sending you these dreams?"

Rooted to my chair, I thought for a minute. Then an inspiration swept through me as if a mighty wind had just blown through that door. Breathless with wonder, I gave her my answer: "God was unlocking the door to his Kingdom so he could reach me in a way I could not ignore. He had something important to say, and he was going to use my dreams to speak to me. I think that God was trying to tell me these initial dreams were meant to make me sit up and pay attention *because more was coming my way.*"

"Yes," Margaret confirmed. "For reasons known only to him, our Holy Father chose this kind of dreaming to communicate with you. Dreaming is and always has been an important form of communication between God and his children. The Bible is full of people he spoke to in their dreams: Jacob, Joseph, Daniel, Ezekiel, Job, Joseph—father of Jesus—and John, just to name a few. When you are at rest, your mind is free of the clutter of your daily life. The Holy Spirit is able to reach through to your very soul to whisper God's Word to you, and if you are patient, he will reveal its meaning. And as God unlocked the door to his Kingdom, he had an important message for you:

> *"Pay attention, my beloved, and listen to me. I have much to teach you."*

"So, my girl, your dreams now move between the earthly and spiritual realms. God has given you the gift of 'eyes that see,' and he is revealing important truths. Soon, we will delve into your sacred dreams. But first, there is something else you need to share. God has graced you with another gift of the Spirit, has he not?"

"Oh," I whispered. "His voice. That still, small *voice.*"

"Ah, yes, child, the most powerful voice in the universe." Margaret nodded meaningfully. "God has also given you 'ears that hear.'"

Eye of the Storm

And he said, "Go out and stand on the mount before the Lord." And behold, the Lord passed by, and a great and strong wind tore the mountains and broke in pieces the rocks before the Lord, but the Lord was not in the wind. And after the wind an earthquake, but the Lord was not in the earthquake. And after the earthquake a fire, but the Lord was not in the fire. And after the fire the sound of a low whisper. And when Elijah heard it, he wrapped his face in his cloak and went out and stood at the entrance of the cave.

1 KINGS 19:11–13

A strong wind began to blow through the yard and tugged at the large umbrella over our table. Margaret turned and looked toward the northwest, and I heard her say softly, "Here it comes." My eyes followed the direction of her gaze and I saw a sky filled with angry black clouds. A summer cloudburst was fast approaching. A loud rumble of thunder filled the air; and with that Cody, Hannah, and Isabel raced in from the back of the yard at something approaching warp speed.

Laughing, Margaret shouted above the wind and thunder,

"We had better take cover on the porch, Jenn! You get the dogs and I'll put down the umbrella!"

I corralled the dogs, and we hurried to the porch, meeting up with Margaret just before the deluge let loose. The covered porch was deep and wide, providing ample shelter from the rain and wind, so we sat down in a couple of rocking chairs to watch and wait it out. Cody frantically pawed his way into our angel friend's lap, and the two smaller dogs jumped up into mine and snuggled in close. Neither of us had any lap left over.

Margaret smiled. "Well, isn't this cozy."

For nearly half an hour, we sat rocking quietly while the storm blew, boomed, and poured out its fury. Finally spent, the clouds broke apart and the warm sun reemerged, creating a landscape glistening with raindrops.

"Storms have always intrigued me," Margaret said with a sigh. "They can be so powerful, and yet they always pass. Many storms leave destruction in their wake, but that mercifully passes, too, and is replaced by healing, strength, and beauty nurtured by the storm's elements. It's like the storms we experience in life. Don't you agree, Jenn?"

"I suppose," I answered hesitantly, unsure of where my friend was going with this point. I began to have an inkling . . .

Margaret turned in her chair to face me directly, her blue eyes looking into mine. "There is a part of your story we have not yet discussed, Jenn, and it's time. I want you to tell me about the period of your life shortly after you dreamed of the child with the heart condition. You were in your late twenties."

My stomach dropped, and I instinctively clutched the two little dogs in my lap and held them closer to me. "Yes, ma'am, I know what you're referring to." I sighed sadly. "I was hoping to skip over this part."

"This is one of the reasons I was sent to guide you on this journey, my sweet girl," said Margaret gently. "This difficult period of your life is an important part of who you are, and it was a time when your Heavenly Father was speaking more powerfully to you than ever before."

It was clear Margaret was not going to let me off the hook, so I took a deep breath and exhaled. "Okay. Here goes. It was during the late 1980s, and during this period of spiritual awakening, another part of my life was being devastatingly slammed shut. My one and *only* plan for my life was to be a wife and mother. Period. I wanted to be just like my own mother, who is wonderful, caring, and nurturing. For years my husband and I tried to have children with no results and the doctors could never say why. I saw infertility specialists, tried various procedures, and despised every second of it. Something that should have been so natural and loving had become clinical and stressful, physically as well as financially. We did not have the money to try the horrendously expensive in vitro fertilization procedure. My friends were all having children and were busy raising their families. I felt so incredibly sad and left out. I stopped seeing many of my friends with children and could not bring myself to attend any of the baby showers I was invited to. In my attempt to mitigate my pain, separating myself from my friends only served to bring on a whole new wave of anguish.

"While all this was going on, I was completely unaware that I was suffering from a thyroid imbalance caused by another benign tumor, which was later successfully removed. These factors combined to play havoc with my emotions, my health, and my marriage. There were no support groups for this kind of thing back then—no one wanted to talk about infertility. My life spun out of control, and I made hurtful choices. My marriage ended—thankfully not bitterly—and both of us moved on with our lives. I was so ashamed and devastated. I was not at all prepared to have my dreams so thoroughly swept away from me, and guess what? *I became very angry with God.* No God could love me and let this happen to me. I prayed and prayed and *prayed* for God to fix things so I could have children, but my prayers were met with absolute silence. So I quit talking to him."

Margaret reached over and placed her hand on my arm. Her eyes expressed a deep empathy, and I knew she had been a witness to all that had happened.

"You went through a terrible storm, Jennifer. I watched what it was like for you, and I grieved along with you. You were lost in the thunder and the wind and the rain, and you could not find God."

"That is a really good description, Margaret. I can give you a little mental picture of what it felt like to be me. When I sat in the bathtub as a little girl, I used to love pulling the drain plug and watching a mini cyclone form as the water was sucked down the drain. Well, I felt like I had been sucked up by that cyclone and thoroughly ripped and torn from all that I knew. I watched as my dreams swirled down the drain. I felt like I couldn't breathe for a very long time. But finally, like you said, the storm passed. I began to try to live my life again, but I still felt terribly lost and sad. And I still wasn't talking to God.

"And that is when the most incredible thing happened, Margaret. When I quit talking to him, *he began talking to me!*

"The first time he did so was the first and only time, so far, that I have heard his voice aloud while awake. I was lying in bed, alone, devastated and trying hard to catch the sleep that had been eluding me. My thoughts spun in my head so fast I could barely keep up. *What am I going to do now? Why did this happen to me? How can I go through life without children and grandchildren? Who will ever want me for a wife?* And that is when I heard, out of the darkness, as if someone was standing right next to my bed, *'Jennifer!'* The voice was loud and startled me into complete silence. All those thoughts instantly evaporated, and I was left with the feeling that God was right there in the room, and he was telling me to just *stop, breathe, trust.* And I did just that, because quite frankly, I didn't know what else to do.

"Then, something began to happen that I've never fully understood. Now that God had my attention again, he began to talk to me in my dreams. I dreamt about my friends, sister, cousins—women who were close to me. In these dreams, a voice would announce that the person I was dreaming about was pregnant. And they were! I was given this knowledge well before their pregnancies were made public. I had never experienced this kind of 'announcing' in a dream before. And I was completely astounded. I mean, here I was, miserable about being childless, and God was giving me dreams about pregnancies. It really felt like a cruel cosmic joke, and it made me sad. That is the part I don't understand, Margaret. Why do you suppose this happened?"

Margaret smiled. "God wasn't trying to make you sad, Jenn. You had stopped listening to him, and these dreams got you listening again, didn't they?"

"Yes, they did," I admitted.

"Child," Margaret said tenderly, "even in the midst of your pain, God was letting you know that he was still there and he had something to say to you. I know it didn't seem like it at the time, but hearing his voice was an important new gift for you."

"Well," I said thoughtfully, "I guess that makes sense. This voice, this announcing, was something I could not ignore. I admit I had not forgiven God yet, but I do agree with you, Margaret . . . I *was* listening again."

"Our Father is most amazing in his persistence, isn't he, dear one?" Margaret smiled wistfully. "This was a crucially important time for you because your Heavenly Father was teaching you how to *recognize his voice*. You needed to know that whenever you are lost or are in the depths of despair, God's quiet voice—the voice that spoke the entire creation into being—will guide you safely back into his loving embrace. I am so glad you began to pay attention to him again."

"I am very glad God was persistent with me," I agreed. "I was so angry and disappointed with him that I am not sure how I would have come back to him on my own. I feel rather ashamed about that."

Margaret nodded, understanding. "That happens a lot. It is a natural tendency for people to blame God when things don't work out the way they expect. But you know what? It is *okay* to be angry with God. He is *God*. He can take it! He would much rather you come to him in your anger and despair than to turn away from him. During this painful chapter of your life, God was always right there. And this is what his still, small voice was trying to tell you:

> *"Most cherished of my heart, I am in the quiet eye of every storm you will go through. When you are caught up in one of life's storms, run to me, dear one, not away from me."*

A giant lump had formed in my throat, and I wasn't able to speak. I felt completely humbled and so very much loved at that moment. As tears welled in my eyes and threatened to spill over, I simply nodded my head.

Margaret reached over and patted my arm. "Now, Jenn, I need to leave you for a little while. I would like to meet you back here this evening after dark, for there is something special we are going to explore together."

With a mysterious gleam in her eyes, Margaret gently removed Cody from her lap and headed out into the glistening wet grass. As she stepped into the butterfly garden, her shimmering yellow gown melted into the yellow lantana flowers, and she disappeared.

Savior

In the beginning the Word already existed. The Word was
with God, and the Word was God. He existed in the
beginning with God. God created everything through him,
and nothing was created except through him. The Word
gave life to everything that was created, and his life brought
light to everyone. The light shines in the darkness, and the
darkness can never extinguish it.

JOHN 1:1–5

Faces of precious family and friends looked back at me through
the many framed photos that decorated my office. I spent the afternoon upstairs in this tranquil space, preparing a Bible study
lesson I would be leading next week. I thought about these faces,
as well as the lovely women who were joining me on this year-
long study journey at church, and found myself in a spontaneous
moment of thankful prayer for the presence of each and every
one of these people in my life. They had stretched me, encouraged me, strengthened me, and loved me. Their faithful friendship had been a true earthly representation of the grace of God.
I reflected on the people in my life who had told me they didn't
want to join a church, that they could just as well find God in the

woods, at the ocean, or in the mountains. I may have agreed with that idea years ago because I, too, found God in all of these places. But through the years, my experience with the unfailing love and support of my church family had shown me the priceless value of a community of faith. Remembering the morning's conversation with my angel, I wished I had had the gift of a godly fellowship of believers those many years ago when I felt so isolated and alone.

The shadows of the evening steadily crept though my office windows as I worked, and soon it was dark. I had lost track of the time since I did not have to stop to prepare dinner—Guy was attending a monthly dinner meeting with colleagues. I quickly realized it was time for another meeting with my angel! I hurried downstairs and stepped onto the patio, looking in the direction of the garden where I last saw Margaret. *Any minute now*, I thought. *I wonder what Margaret has planned for tonight?* She had ever so gently guided me into discovering new and precious truths in each one of our conversations. This morning's conversation had included a topic that had always been acutely painful for me, yet at its conclusion I felt profoundly loved.

The night was warm and peaceful. All the busy-ness and noise of the day had been put to rest. I listened to the faint rustle of the breeze and the soft music of my wind chimes. Then, next to the statue of St. Francis, a faint shimmer of light appeared. It grew steadily brighter, and I again saw the faint outline of wings—my angel was back! Margaret stepped from the garden and came to stand by my side. She smelled faintly of white roses.

"Did you enjoy your day, Jenn?" she asked.

"Yes, I did," I replied. "I did a lot of reflecting on what we talked about and how God's voice called me back to him."

She smiled and I noticed that mysterious gleam again. "We are going to continue our conversation, and I am so excited because tonight is all about the wonder of his love." She motioned over to our chairs by the fire pit. "Let's go sit."

We settled into our two chairs, looking out into the backyard, and sat for a few moments in silence, letting the quiet of the night seep into our hearts. The scent of gardenias was heavy in the air, and little tree frogs began to sing, creating a rhythmic chorus in the darkness.

After a while Margaret spoke. "Look at all those stars." She sighed, leaning her head back against the chair and lifting her face to the heavens. "So many beautiful points of light." She turned her head and looked at me, and with a soft voice she said, "You had a personal encounter with the Original Source of this light, didn't you?"

"Yes," I breathed, looking up at the star-filled sky. "I sure did. I met him in the darkest place I have ever been."

"Tell me," Margaret prodded gently.

My heart quickened as I began to tell Margaret the story of a night and a meeting arranged by the Almighty himself.

"The agony of the years of my infertility and then a failed marriage took a deep toll on me. I felt so far away from God and so far away from myself. I had no idea how to get back to the happy, confident young woman I had been so long ago. I began to see a therapist, who did help me to put things in perspective a bit, but I was still so incredibly *sad*. Then, one night, soon after hearing God speak my name by my bedside, I went to bed and dreamed a dream that changed my life."

As my dream begins, I am walking in a cold, very dark desert. There are no stars, and I am afraid. I don't know what I am afraid of, but it has something to do with being out after dark. For some reason, it is very important to be home after the sun has set, or I will be in danger. I move quickly toward my house in the desert, a clay dwelling with open-air, arched windows. It reminds me of something one might see in old Jerusalem. As I walk on the cold sand, my fear rises to an almost panicked level. I have to get to my house soon, but my house is dark, and I am also afraid of what the darkness inside the house might hold for me. As I finally approach, I am amazed to see a hand placing a candle in the window. No one is supposed to be there! I feel instant relief at that little point of light—it is the only light I can see for miles around. I enter my home. It has a dirt floor, and there is no furniture. I look across the room toward the window, and what I see astonishes me. There, standing in a shimmering gold light that encompasses his whole being, is Jesus! I fall to my knees before him in absolute wonder. His hand is still on the candleholder in the window as if he is still holding it to light my way. I cannot see the details of his face clearly because of the incredible, shimmering gold light, but I instantly know him. He smiles and his voice says to me, "I will always be here for you, Jen-

nifer." With that, he begins to shimmer even more and starts to fade. The gold shimmers are dispersing in an ever-widening pattern until they engulf the whole room, swirling around me. The very air I breathe is full of him, effervescent. As I breathe in, it feels as if I have been dropped into a very bubbly glass of champagne and am breathing in the liquid bubbles. Then the room becomes quiet. He is gone. But I am no longer afraid. When I awaken from my dream, I feel, for the first time in a very long time, that things are going to be okay. And even better, I also know I have just met my Savior, the Light of the World.

My beautiful angel and I sat gazing at the stars in silence after I finished my story. Even after all these years, the memory of my meeting with Jesus is still so powerful that it can bring me to my knees.

Margaret's voice gently interrupted my thoughts. "Jenn, have you ever thought about why your dream took place in a desert?"

I thought for a minute. "I guess I always assumed it was because I felt so lonely and left out, just as the desert seems a very lonely place," I answered.

Margaret nodded thoughtfully. Then she said quietly, "The desert is also a very barren place, Jenn. Barren and seemingly lifeless. But when the rains come and the desert is soaked in water, it blooms. Does this resonate with you?"

I winced at her use of the word *barren*. "Oh, Margaret, that word still distresses me. But, yes, it does resonate with me.

I struggled so much with being childless and hated the word *barren* every time I encountered it. My life seemed empty, without purpose."

"I know, dear child, and what you need to realize is that *you were that desert*. You felt barren and lifeless, until you met Jesus in your dream. Then a miracle happened. You met the Source of Light and Living Water. You soaked in his very essence, and you bloomed."

As I let her words sink in, a memory from my childhood sprang forth. I had actually seen the Arizona desert in bloom after a rainy spring. The cactus flowers were so beautiful. I knew Margaret was right.

"I guess I did bloom, Margaret. Things really began to change for me. I regained the confidence I'd once had and began picking up the pieces of my life. I had a wonderfully supportive family, a good job, got back in touch with friends, and within a few years married my Guy. And I even got a chance to be a mom by helping to raise his son. I gave my all to a special little boy named Jason who is now a grown-up, independent young man.

"To this very day, I am so very touched and humbled to know that in my darkness, my Lord reached out to me and found me. He knew how very much I needed him, even when I didn't realize it. He really does not give up on you."

"No, he does not," agreed Margaret. "I wish more people realized this. Many feel they are unworthy of God's love, because they have made poor decisions or have made a mess of their lives. Some feel that God doesn't even know they exist. But what people need to understand is that they *are* worthy *because they are his children*. God put each and every person here on this earth and cares deeply for them. All you have to do is seek him. He will find you and meet you where you are.

"Your dream reminds me of a biblical parallel, Jenn. Do you remember the story in Exodus, of the Israelites on the last night of their captivity in Egypt? On that night, God sent the final and most deadly plague against the pharaoh and the Egyptians in order to demonstrate his power as the one true God and to convince the pharaoh to let the Israelites leave the country. The Israelites were instructed to place the blood of a lamb on the doorposts of their homes and to stay inside. That night was dark and terrifying, and they were very afraid. At midnight, the harbinger of death began to creep through the neighborhoods. And then something wonderful happened. It was as if the blood smeared on the doorposts suddenly blazed and pierced the darkness like the brightest of stars, repulsing the evil plague so that it passed over their homes, and the Israelites were spared the deaths of their firstborns. God was the deliverer of his people. And our beloved Jesus is the New Testament Lamb, who shed his blood for all people, saving them from the darkness forever."

"The story of the Exodus is one of my favorites," I replied with a wistful smile. "And I do see the parallel. Jesus, the Lamb of God, certainly did deliver me when he found me in the terrifying night of my dream and led me home with his Light. The Light repelled the fear, the darkness, and the oppression I had been feeling for so long."

"Indeed it did, dear one," Margaret agreed. "And as you slept, your Savior personally delivered this promise to you:

"I am always here for you, my child. No darkness is too dark, no circumstance is too dire for me to walk into with my Light and free you."

My heart swelled as I listened to these words, remembering the intensity of Jesus' presence in my dream. There was no doubt in my mind . . . *no one* is beyond the reach of the saving grace of our precious Savior.

"After I had this dream, I really made an effort to return fully to God, paying attention to what he said to me in my dreams. And as I did, I noticed a new gift was emerging. I began to hear him while I was awake. Not out loud, but what I call an inside voice. It is a voice that speaks inside me, clearly and concisely—only a few words at a time."

"I know that voice well, dear child," said Margaret softly.

We sat contentedly for a few moments, listening to the growing multitude of chirping voices provided by the frogs and crickets. Then my dear angel stood and stretched, and I knew our evening had drawn to a close.

"This night has been special, Jenn. I have loved sitting here under the stars with you and hearing about your encounter with Jesus. The starry night sky is a wonderful reminder to humanity of the Light that pierces the darkness.

"You need to get some rest now. Sleep sweetly tonight and I

will see you in the morning. Tomorrow, let's speak more about the Almighty's voice. Good night, dear one."

"Good night, Margaret," I replied, stifling a yawn.

I leaned back in my chair and watched as she slowly faded into the shadows and disappeared. Then I turned my eyes once more to the heavens and whispered "Good night" to my Savior— my beautiful, shimmering Light.

Whispered Blessings

And the Lord called Samuel again the third time. And he
arose and went to Eli and said, "Here I am, for you called
me." Then Eli perceived that the Lord was calling the young
man. Therefore Eli said to Samuel, "Go, lie down, and if he
calls you, you shall say, 'Speak, Lord, for your servant
hears.'" So Samuel went and lay down in his place.
And the Lord came and stood, calling as at other times,
"Samuel! Samuel!" And Samuel said, "Speak, for your
servant hears."

1 SAMUEL 3:8–10

The next morning dawned as only one in southeast Texas
could—sunny, hot, and steamy. In anticipation of Margaret's arrival, I carried two cups of coffee out onto the patio and set them
on the garden table. I then turned my attention to the Frisbee in-
sistently bumping into the back of my legs. Cody stood there, determined that we get a few throws in before Margaret arrived. I
marvel at how he can communicate very effectively without
words! After several long runs through the deep backyard, Cody
happily jumped into the pool to cool off. I settled comfortably at
the table and closed my eyes, listening to the sounds of the morn-

ing. Already, the cicadas were buzzing, calling to one another across the neighboring yards, a distinctive sign that we were deep into summer. This is when my husband and I love to sit and enjoy this lovely space together . . . as the day awakens. Its quiet beauty infuses us with a peace that doesn't come from this world. I felt a twinge of melancholy tug at my heart. Guy had come home late last night, packed a suitcase, and headed out to catch a red-eye flight for a last-minute business trip. This trip would take him overseas, which meant that he would be gone at least a week. My heart was already growing homesick for him.

"This is the day the Lord has made, let us rejoice and be glad in it!"

I jumped in my chair, eyes flying open. There was my beautiful angel, laughing and standing behind me. She looked radiant. Today her silver-blue gown had swirls of pink in it, matching the slight pink flush of her cheeks. The diamond-like material shimmered in the sun.

"Good morning, Margaret."

"And a good morning to you, sweet girl," she replied. "Our Father sends you his dearest love and is so pleased with our progress so far."

More goose bumps. To receive such a personal message from my Lord filled me with awe.

Margaret gracefully swept into the chair next to me and settled herself in. She gave a little squeak of elation as she spied the coffee on the table and indulged in a long, slightly noisy, delicious sip. I tried hard to suppress a giggle. This angel and her coffee cracked me up!

As Margaret finally set her cup back down on the table, she turned her twinkling blue eyes on me. I knew we were in for another fascinating conversation. "Last night we began to talk about a new way God was making himself known to you—through an internal voice. Since humans are exposed to so much *noise* in their daily lives, this can be a very difficult gift to discern. Can you tell me how you have been able to do so?"

"It *has* been difficult to discern," I agreed. "I believe a lot of people have this gift, yet they do not recognize it as God's voice. It can come as an urge to call someone, to check on a friend, to pray for someone. You can sense danger nearby—all the little quiet nudges that many simply attribute to thought, intuition, or imagination. As I mentioned last night, when I hear God's voice, it is an inside, internal voice. *A whisper.* I do not hear him speaking out loud like you and I are doing right now. And he uses very few words. The way I recognize the difference between his voice and my own thoughts is that his voice comes when I least expect it—when my mind is occupied by something else. It interrupts. It is clear, concise, and cuts to my very core, pushing aside all other thoughts. Also, his message will often repeat—most likely because the first time I unfortunately have either misidentified, questioned, or ignored it. In this case, he usually persists until I finally listen and, if necessary, obey."

"Well stated, Jenn," said Margaret, "and if you don't mind, I'd like to add something I think is important. A simple way to recognize God's voice is to see it is a Divine prompt that will bring *healing, comfort,* or *blessing* to you or to someone else. And if this prompt requires obedience, that obedience will glorify God."

As I let this angelic wisdom sink in for a moment, I recalled an intriguing story about obedience. "It always inspires me, Margaret, to hear the stories of others who *do* recognize God's quiet voice and are obedient to it. A friend once shared a story with me about how she was awakened in the middle of the night by a strong urging to pray for her son, who was many miles away in a big city. Worried, she tried to reach him by phone but was unsuccessful. So she did as the urging instructed. She prayed and prayed. The next morning she learned her son had been the victim of a mugging but, thankfully, he was all right. I'm sure my friend's prayers had a lot to do with her son's survival, and I know she has lifted many heartfelt praises to God for his intervention in her son's life-threatening encounter. God most certainly was glorified in this story of prayerful obedience."

Margaret clasped her hands to her heart. "Yes, he was. That was a wonderful example. And now I want you to tell me one of *your* stories about hearing God's voice. I believe you have several that are particularly meaningful," she hinted with a knowing smile.

"I do," I said. "The first happened several years ago. I had my yearly mammogram and was called back for an ultrasound. During the ultrasound, the radiologist came into the room and asked me if I knew about a mass in my right breast. I replied that yes, I had had it for twenty years or so. It was a suspected fibroid tumor, and no one had ever seemed too concerned about it. He then suggested it should be biopsied. Grudgingly, I agreed, but my normally active imagination went into overdrive, and I was scared to death. I underwent the procedure and began the five-

to seven-day wait for the results. I was a mess. I could not con-
centrate on anything. I eventually decided to try to go about my
normal routine as much as possible to keep my mind occupied.
One morning, while applying my makeup, two words suddenly
interrupted and said quite clearly in my heart, *'blessed assurance.'* I was surprised, to say the least, but it did give me a little
bit of comfort. As the day progressed, every time I started to
worry again, those same two words would interrupt. Several
days later, I still did not have a pathology report, but I headed to
Methodist Hospital in Houston where I volunteered as a lay
minister. A lay minister is a non-clergy person trained by the
chaplain or spiritual care department to visit with patients—to
listen to them and to pray with them.

"I was assigned to a medical floor and the transplant unit.
My mentor chaplain was a wonderful woman named Michelle. I
stopped in to see her before I went up to the transplant unit to
begin my visits. She asked me how I was doing, and I broke
down in tears and told her what was going on. When I told her
that I kept hearing two words in my heart, she asked me what
they were. When I told her 'blessed assurance,' her reaction was
amazing! She looked at me stunned and said, 'Jennifer, that is my
favorite hymn!'

"*Hymn?* I had no idea what she meant. She jumped up and
pulled a hymnal from her bookshelf and turned to it. Sure
enough, there was the hymn, 'Blessed Assurance.' We read the
hymn together and then we prayed together. The words of the
hymn were such *comfort*. What a healing moment that was.
How wonderful that my Father in heaven would use the words

from a hymn to speak to me when he knows music is so dear to my heart. I just knew things would be okay. And later in the day I learned that my biopsy results were benign."

Margaret sighed. "It is not surprising to me that he used the words of a hymn to speak words of comfort to you. *He created your inmost being. He knit you together in your mother's womb.* He knows your heart and loves you so very much, precious one."

My heart swelled with love as I heard her words. "God spoke to me again through music several years later. Guy and I had moved away from our friends and beloved church home in League City and relocated to The Woodlands area north of Houston. It was a good move for us, but I missed my friends and church family terribly and did not know a single person up here. I began a search for a new church while Guy was traveling overseas. I visited several churches but did not find anything to fit me and my spiritual and worship needs. When Guy returned home, he suggested that we try The Woodlands United Methodist Church near our home. I had been there once for a week as a delegate to the Texas Annual Conference of the United Methodist Church several years before. This is a huge, eleven-thousand-member church with a large sanctuary.

"I was intimidated by the size of this church and confided to my husband that I was afraid I would not be able to find my way among so many people. How would I ever get to know anyone in a church this size? So Guy suggested we start by attending a smaller, early service in the church's lovely chapel.

"Sunday morning arrived, and while I was busy getting dressed, a couple of words suddenly planted themselves into my heart and mind: *'How beautiful.'* Why, thank you, Father! I thought playfully, thinking he had just paid me a compliment."

Another very unangel-like snicker bubbled from the chair next to me. I glanced over to see Margaret rolling her eyes.

"I know, I know, just my vanity rearing its ugly head," I said quickly, before she could. "I figured out pretty quickly that those words meant something else, because they kept repeating over the next half hour or so as we continued to get ready to go to church. When we arrived at the church, the service was about to start, so we quickly found seats. Not too far into the service, a musician began to play a flute solo. It was such a lovely melody, and I glanced down at my bulletin to see what the song was titled. Imagine my astonishment to see printed in the bulletin the words *How Beautiful*.

"I leaned over and whispered to Guy, 'You know those words I told you were running through my head this morning while I was getting ready? It is the name of this song . . . look! Isn't that *weird*?'

"Guy leaned over to me with a grin and whispered, *'No,* Jenn, *you're* weird!'

"My sweet husband is used to these revelations of mine, bless his heart.

"And the morning just kept getting more amazing. The scripture reading from Mark chapter five, verses twenty-five to thirty-four, told the story of a long-suffering woman in a crowd of people surrounding Jesus who reached out in faith to touch Jesus' cloak. Jesus felt the power leave him and asked, 'Who touched me?' When the woman acknowledged her action, Jesus told her, 'Your faith has made you well.' That has always been one of my very favorite scriptures. Then, during his sermon, the pastor told a story about his grandmother who experienced visions, and he described an encounter she had with her son who had died. I remember him saying something to the effect that he didn't know how we all felt about people having visions, but his grandmother believed what she experienced was real. It was as if he was speaking to me directly, and I felt like Jesus was sitting right next to me, saying, 'See, Jennifer, this church is where you need to be. I have given you several signs today that you can be comfortable and find purpose here.'

"Well, he didn't have to whack *me* over the head with a two-by-four anymore. I got his message loud and clear and felt humbled and at peace that this would be my new church home and that my Lord had selected it for me. And I will tell you that being a member of this church has been an overwhelming *blessing* to me and has helped me to grow as a Christian. I joined the choir and met many wonderful new friends and have been able to get back to leading Bible study, which has been a passion of mine for many years."

"Oh, my dear Jennifer, God has a specific plan for your life, and you are seeing it unfold before your very eyes. It is so important to realize that you are where he wants you to be at this moment in time. And I am so thankful you have learned to listen to what he says to you," said Margaret. She leaned back in her chair and lifted her face to the sun. "In fact, the very angels of heaven rejoice when God's people learn to listen and obey his voice, as his message can have eternal significance in the lives of his children."

Margaret then turned to me, and her face had taken on a serious look. "You have a story that is a poignant illustration of how important it is to listen and *obey*. Do you know the experience I am referring to?"

"I do. It was one of the most humbling experiences of my life."

The memory of this encounter still tugs at my heart. "The experience you are referring to took place when, again, I was at Methodist Hospital doing my lay ministry visits. Before beginning, I routinely prayed a short prayer, asking God to empty me so I could fully serve him and the patients I visited. My inspiration for this was in Philippians when Christ 'emptied himself, by taking the form of a servant.' Without first laying all of my own needs, concerns, and to-do lists at his feet, I would not be able to give all of myself to the patients and their needs. My prayer always ended with a request that God would guide me to those needing his comfort that day. I have many examples of the wonderful ways he answered this prayer, every single time I served as a lay minister, steering me to particular patient rooms, giving me appropriate words of prayer—the list is long. But this one particular experience will stay with me forever in its example of how he used me to help minister to one of his beloved children.

"I completed my rounds on the medical floor, taking longer than usual, and I arrived on the transplant unit already emotionally weary. This was a very special floor. The patients I visited with could be in one of three different stages: awaiting a transplant, immediate post-transplant, or experiencing problems with or rejection of their transplant. I was issued a daily census listing the patient names and room numbers and began my journey around the huge U-shaped floor. I had a couple of visits, but many patients were either sleeping or absent from their rooms, so I began to feel that my day would soon be over. I headed down the backstretch of the U shape and paused at the room of a patient whose name I did not recognize. The door was slightly ajar, and when I looked in, there were several physicians in the room. Protocol indicated that I skip a room when a physician is in attendance, so I went on my way and ended up at the end of the floor. Whew! My day was done, and I was tired. I headed to the elevators and pressed the Down button. Suddenly, a very strong inside voice commanded—and I mean *commanded*: '*Go back to that room!*'

"*Oh, come on!* I thought. *Not now. I am really tired and that room was full of doctors.* I pressed Down again. Once more the voice commanded, '*Turn around and go back to that room!*' Okay, this time the voice sounded a little mad, so I let out an exasperated sigh, whirled around, and went back to the patient's room. To my surprise, the room was now empty except for the patient.

"I knocked softly on the open door and walked in, finding the patient sitting in a chair next to his bed. When I looked at him, I recognized him as a man I had visited with in prior weeks. 'Well, hello!' I said. 'How are you doing today?'

"'Oh!' he exclaimed. 'I am so glad you came back to see me. I saw you walk by when all the doctors were here a few minutes ago, and I was afraid you might not come back.'

"Now, this is when I started to realize God was up to something special. I remembered this man had been on a waiting list for a heart transplant. He had some sort of artificial implant that was keeping his heart going and knew each day was a race against time. The news the doctors had just given him was not very encouraging. We talked a long time about his feelings, and he asked me to pray with him before I left. He was such a dear man, and together we participated in a very personal time of prayer with our Lord. When we were through, he held my hands and thanked me and asked me to come back and see him when I returned the next week.

"When I did return, I did not see this man's name on the census, so I asked about him. I was told very gently by the nurse that he'd had a major stroke the morning after I had visited with him the week before and had gone into a coma. After several days he died, never regaining consciousness. My heart was broken for that sweet little man. But I was overwhelmed by what the Lord had done for his beloved child. He made sure that this man had been ministered to and had the opportunity to go to his Lord in prayer before he died. And he used me to help make it possible. I was completely and utterly humbled, as well as privately ashamed at my initial reaction to my Lord's command to go back to that room. I am *so* very glad I decided to listen and obey his voice that day!"

Margaret looked over at me, and I saw that her face was streaming with tears. She smiled a little crookedly and made a sign with her hand as if to say *keep going*, since she was too emotional to speak at the moment.

So I continued with a thought that had been on my mind for a while.

"I know there have been many times in my life when I have either completely missed or, even worse, just ignored God's voice. So often I have felt an urge to act, to give someone an unexpected hug, or heard a whisper to call someone, yet just passed it off as my imagination. I wonder how many opportunities to minister to someone I have missed by doing so."

Margaret gave me a tiny smile and her voice quavered with emotion. "Can you imagine, my dear, what this world would be like if all people listened for the Father's voice and acted upon it? *It would be like heaven on earth.*"

She reached over and took my hand in hers. "God is constantly speaking to all of his Creation, and isn't it marvelous that the most powerful voice in the universe needs only to *whisper*? Hear, Jenn, what your Creator whispers to you now:

"Listen to me, beloved child, and do as I ask. You do not have to understand why. Each and every time, when my voice is heard and obeyed, someone is blessed."

After a quiet pause, Margaret slowly got up from her chair, brushing away the tears still streaming down her cheeks. Clearing her throat, she said, "Forgive my Kleenex moment, Jenn. Your stories were wonderful examples of how and why God speaks to his children. I am always so moved when I see how our Father works in the lives of his beloved. He loves all of you so much. Now, if you will excuse me, I need to go attend to my rather tearstained eyes and face." With that, she hurried across the patio to the back door and let herself into the house.

I sat for a moment, wondering if I should go inside and help her. But then I decided that Margaret *was* an angel, after all, and had been looking after me all these years, so she probably didn't need any assistance from me. I leaned back in my chair, absorbing the sunshine, and watched a couple of bluebirds investigate an empty birdhouse in the yard. I wondered if they were getting ready to raise a new brood of chicks as they had earlier in the spring. The warmth of the sun made me sleepy and I closed my eyes for a minute. *Hmm,* I thought, as I began to drift off . . . *Margaret said God speaks to all of Creation. I wonder if he speaks to bluebirds . . .*

3-D Vision

In the last days, God says, I will pour out my Spirit on all people. Your sons and daughters will prophesy, your young men will see visions, your old men will dream dreams. Even on my servants, both men and women, I will pour out my Spirit in those days and they will prophesy. I will show wonders in the heaven above and signs on the earth below, blood and fire and billows of smoke. The sun will be turned to darkness and the moon to blood before the coming of the great and glorious day of the Lord. And everyone who calls on the name of the Lord will be saved.

ACTS 2:17–21

"All better now," exclaimed my angel as she strolled out the back door and onto the patio, abruptly ending my catnap. "How do I look? Nice?" I turned to look at Margaret and laughed out loud. There she stood, posing dramatically with one hand on her hip, an exaggerated smile showing all of her perfect, small white teeth, and wearing an enormous pair of black horn-rimmed sunglasses. She looked ridiculous. I got up and joined her.

"What in the world?" I laughed. "*Where* did you get those silly glasses?"

"Don't you recognize them? They were on your kitchen counter next to the box of tissues."

"Oh yeah," I exclaimed as I looked closer. "Those are the 3-D glasses I brought home from the movie Guy and I saw the other night on our dinner-and-a-movie date. Why are you wearing those? There isn't anything unusual you can see with them right now. *Is there?*"

Margaret beamed and linked her arm through mine, leading me back to our chairs overlooking the yard. We sat, and she pulled out another pair of glasses from the folds of her gown—she must have found both pairs inside. "Here," she said, "put these on."

Giggling, I put on my 3-D glasses and looked at Margaret. We must have looked really goofy sitting out here in these enormous black glasses. Margaret giggled, too, and then, oh my, a hilarious little snort escaped from her nose. We both dissolved in laughter so hard it made my sides ache.

"Okay, seriously now," said Margaret, trying to put a solemn look on her face. Somehow she actually achieved it while I sat there grinning ear to ear.

"I wanted us to wear these to illustrate a point. When you went to the movie the other night, you had to wear these glasses to see a dimension hidden from your normal vision. Right?"

"Yes," I replied. "And it was really cool. Everything looked so realistic and clear. The characters looked as if they were standing right there in front of me."

"That's right," said Margaret. "If you had tried to watch the movie without the glasses, the images on the screen would have been blurred. You would have missed the clarity and wonder a third dimension provides as revealed by the 3-D glasses. Jenn, do you remember our earlier discussion about heavenly inter- sections?"

I nodded.

"Today," Margaret continued, "our journey brings us to the heart of one of these intersections—the place where heaven meets you in your dreams to reveal deep and hidden truths. You might say that you wear spiritual 3-D glasses while you sleep, my dear, because you are a Divine dreamer. This gift carries an anointing of the Holy Spirit and should be taken seriously. Your dreams can include prophecy, warning, instruction, and revela- tion, and while some dreams may be private, others may be shared as the Spirit leads."

More goose bumps. My heart constricted from the depth of emotion this subject triggers within me. It is a gift I have held close to my heart for many years and have shared it with very few people.

"Margaret," I said softly, "these dreams are very special to me, and I want so badly to understand what God is trying to say to me. Sometimes there are things in my dreams that are obvi- ous and easy to understand, but for the most part, well, you know me and how long it takes for me to *get it*," I said with a small laugh.

"I think I might be able to help shed light on what you do not understand," Margaret said, smiling, "but before we get to that, I'd like you to tell me a little bit about what it is like to expe- rience Divine dreams."

"Well," I began thoughtfully, "my very first clue that I have experienced a Divine dream is that the realism of the dream is extraordinary and the memory does not fade as normal dreams do. I can recall every detail, even after many years, as if I were watching a movie. Sometimes I am just an observer, and sometimes I'm an active participant. But in both cases, there is the presence of an intellect other than my own. It is deep, pervasive, and wise. Upon awakening from the dream, I am overcome with the knowledge that I have received a special kind of communication from God. And then comes the hard part . . . figuring out what it means."

"Do you want to know something remarkable, Jenn?" Margaret asked.

I nodded enthusiastically.

"The key to understanding your dreams lives in that beautiful book you hold in your hands every morning. Holy Scripture— the Word of God—is the very source of the truths God is revealing to you in your dreams. I know you have already experienced a few moments of clarity about your dreams while reading your Bible. The deeper you go into the Scriptures, the clearer your understanding will be. You will recognize this truth as we begin to explore your dreams, and you will also discover that Scripture reflects the very character of God. God is not linear. The Bible reveals that he is the God of past, present, and future. You will see that your dreams reflect this.

"And, you must keep in mind that God's Word is a *living Word*. God speaks to you where you are. His truth moves with you, revealing what you need to know at just the right time, as you are ready to receive. Patience is a virtue, child. Understanding the mysteries God reveals to you can take time, and is well worth the wait."

I grudgingly agreed. "I admit to being impatient sometimes when it comes to understanding my dreams because I know that wondrous truths are waiting to be discovered. I can say one thing for certain, though, my angel friend. These Divine dreams have led me to consider there is much more to our everyday existence than meets the eye. I guess you could say God was the original inventor of 3-D vision."

"Oh, my, child, you just might be right about that!" laughed Margaret. "Now hold that thought. I have a perfect story from Second Kings to share with you. It's about when God opened the eyes of Elisha's servant to reveal an incredible sight . . . at just the right time."

When the servant of the man of God got up early the next morning and went outside, there were troops, horses, and chariots everywhere. "Oh, sir, what will we do now?" the young man cried to Elisha. "Don't be afraid!" Elisha told him. "For there are more on our side than on theirs!" Then Elisha prayed, "O Lord, open his eyes and let him see!" The Lord opened the young man's eyes, and when he looked up, he saw that the hillside around Elisha was filled with horses and chariots of fire.

As she finished the story, Margaret's voice trembled with emotion. "Jenn," she said, "God did this very thing for you when he gave you this gift of Divine dreams. As you slept, he spoke this into your heart:

> *"I have opened your eyes, precious child, so that you may see the wonders of my kingdom!"*

"So now let's delve right into these wondrous dreams of yours." Margaret removed her 3-D glasses, leaned back in her chair, let out a deep sigh, and closed her eyes, ready to listen.

I decided to keep my 3-D glasses on while I began to speak of dreams.

Pilgrimage

Blessed are those whose strength is in you,
whose hearts are set on pilgrimage.

PSALM 84:5

As Margaret sat listening contentedly, I related the details of a
dream—a journey to a mysterious mountain.

*I am carrying a small suitcase. I look ahead of me and
realize I am in a very long, winding line of people, all carrying suitcases like me. We are in a beautiful valley. The
line snakes gently over small rolling green hills and leads
to a large mountain ahead, in the distance. I wonder to
myself, Where in the world am I and, more important,
where am I going? I sense the same vague type of mystery
from the people around me, curiously mixed with a feeling of excited anticipation. We smile and nod to one another as we slowly meander along.*

*Suddenly, a man appears directly in front of me wear-
ing jeans and a dark brown T-shirt. The curious thing
about his T-shirt is that it has on it a line of little white*

sheep, which wrap in a band all the way around the shirt, right at chest level. The even more curious thing is that the sheep are moving—as if they, too, are walking in a line. Now, this man is beautiful—absolutely, strikingly beautiful. He has dark hair, a closely trimmed beard and mustache, and eyes that sparkle with such extraordinary radiance and excitement that I can't even tell what color they are. He speaks directly to me, and with a smile reflecting the radiance in his eyes, he exclaims, "Isn't this wonderful? Isn't this exciting?" He then steps aside to give me a view of the mountain ahead of us. People are now streaming up one side of the mountain and down the other, and at the very top of the mountain is Jesus. I guess that this must be an angel speaking with me, and his pure joy and excitement catch like a wildfire in my heart. We are on a journey to see Jesus!

When I finished, Margaret opened her eyes and said, "My goodness, Jenn, what a wonderful dream. I felt like I was right there with you. Thank you. So, tell me your initial impressions of your dream. How did it make you feel?"

"The first thing I remember from when I woke up was that the feelings of joy and anticipation I experienced in the dream were still with me. And the angel with the beautiful smile and eyes, so alive with excitement, is as clear in my memory today as he was twenty or more years ago when I had the dream. Other than that, I really did not understand much about the meaning of this dream until I experienced a particular moment of clarity while studying the Song of Ascents ... " I paused as I was struck by a sudden realization.

"You're right, Margaret. *I was reading Scripture* when I got this moment of clarity."

Margaret just smiled and waited for me to continue.

"Okay, back to my story. The Song of Ascents are fifteen psalms sung by the Israelites as they journeyed to and from Jerusalem three times a year to celebrate Passover and the harvest feasts at the Temple in Jerusalem. This type of journey was called a pilgrimage, and I pictured in my mind large groups of extended families making these pilgrimages together—cooking and camping out by night; riding, walking, and visiting by day—filled with anticipation of arriving in their beloved city and celebrating the harvest feast together in the presence of God. And all the while they sang songs handed down from generation to generation to pass the time and to express the joy of their journey. I realized I had similar memories of my own family travels—singing songs and playing games to pass the time, each of us full of excitement and anticipation of arriving at our destination and the fun awaiting us.

"While studying the Song of Ascents, I vacationed with my husband and parents in Old Orchard Beach, Maine. It was my first visit to Maine, and it was beautiful. The beach was wide and long, the sun bright, and we had many cool breezes, a wonderful respite from the suffocating summer heat of Houston. One morning early in the week, I pulled out my Bible after getting myself settled on the beach. I began to read while other people began filing down to the beach with their chairs and towels and beach bags. It was very quiet—just the sound of the waves of the distant tide. After a while, I began to hear the soft strumming of a guitar accompanied by several voices singing along. I glanced over and saw an ever-growing circle of people sitting in the sand, laughing, talking, and holding their coffee cups, obviously enjoying one another's company. Every once in a while, another person would arrive and was greeted with great joy and big hugs all around. I learned from my parents that this was a large reunion of a French Canadian family. Several of them traveled to this spot every year, but this particular gathering would include many who had not seen each other in years. A big feast was planned later in the week that would include at least fifty family members.

"This was a musical family, and soon other instruments appeared, more voices joined the singing, and they were singing in French. It was so beautiful to listen to that I had a hard time concentrating on my reading. Then I was struck by a most amazing revelation. Isn't this remarkably similar to what was happening in the Song of Ascents, as the Israelites made their pilgrimage to Jerusalem? Families that traveled together, loved one another, and sang together, filled with excitement and anticipation of arriving at their destination, their journey culminating in a great celebration feast . . . a celebration of love? Even I was included, as I had traveled a great distance from Texas to Maine to spend a week with my beloved parents. Suddenly the centuries had melted away, and I was a member of the peoples of the pilgrimage—God's people. As I thought this very thought, a voice inside me said, "*It is all tied together, Jen-*

nifer." My breath caught in my throat. I slammed my study book shut, closed my eyes, and prayed, *Praise you, Father! Thank you.* I opened up my book again and wrote those words and the date on the page."

I paused. Margaret was nodding her head vigorously up and down, looking like she wanted jump in. I let her speak.

"It *is* all tied together, dear one, more than you realize," she said. "First, listen to what Isaiah says about a particular mountain in scripture: 'In days to come the mountain of the Lord's house shall be established as the highest of the mountains, and shall be raised above the hills; all the nations shall stream to it. Many peoples shall come and say, 'Come, let us go up to the mountain of the Lord, to the house of the God of Jacob; that he may teach us his ways and that we may walk in his paths.'"

Margaret smiled as my eyes widened in surprise. *That scripture was a pretty good description of my dream.* She continued.

"Jennifer, your dream reveals several truths about the magnificent journey you are on as you live your life on earth. Your journey begins under the watchful eye of a shepherd, and his joy increases as you move ever closer to the pinnacle in the distance and begin your ascent, because he knows what awaits you at the top. *You, along with countless others throughout the ages, are on a lifelong pilgrimage to discover the Savior—the living source of love, grace, and truth.* Each of you ascends the mountain at your own pace, depending upon the burdens you carry, and as you draw near to the Savior, your perspective begins to change. Hope, joy, and peace no longer seem unattainable. Then, as you meet Christ on the mountaintop, you encounter your future and are forever changed. As you make your way back down the mountain, you are a new creation, a beacon of hope along the path to encourage those just beginning their pilgrimages. And, Jennifer, pilgrimages are *joyful* events! They begin with great anticipation and end with celebratory feasts. It is no wonder the feelings of joy and anticipation remained with you when you awakened."

I loved how my angel was tying all this together. "One of the reasons I was so moved on the beach that day in Maine, Margaret, was because when I realized how similar my own journeys and celebrations were to the pilgrimages and feasts of the ancient peoples I was reading about, I felt really connected to them," I said.

"Actually, you are more connected than you think," said Margaret. "The Old Testament feasts celebrated by God's people throughout the centuries foreshadowed the future, accomplished in the life, death, and resurrection of Jesus. The Old Testament feasts of Passover, Unleavened Bread, and First Fruits are celebrated in early spring. The Feast of Weeks is held in early summer, and the Feast of Tabernacles is held in the fall—the final harvest festival. Your New Testament Christian celebrations of Good Friday, Easter, and Pentecost parallel the Old Testament harvest feasts and are held at the same time of year, in spring and early summer. There is, however, one Old Testament feast that has not yet been celebrated in New Testament times: the Feast of Tabernacles, the final harvest. Only when Christ returns will he gather his people to him in the final harvest. Can you imagine, child, how great *that* celebration feast will be?" Margaret's eyes sparkled, and I was reminded of the angel's sparkling eyes in my dream.

"As you were speaking just now, Margaret, a wonderful picture formed in my mind. I envisioned that the long line of people in my dream streaming to the mountain is like looking down on the Earth from God's point of view. God is watching his beloved children march along the time-line span of the ages from Old Testament days to the present day and into the future. Marching toward him. Standing with many others in an unending line with my suitcase in hand, *I am an active participant in this ancient tradition.* And one glorious day, all of us, all nations, will come to the mountain of the Lord, just as Isaiah has foretold. That will be a marvelous celebration indeed. I can see why the angel in my dream was so excited for us!"

"About that angel, Jenn," said Margaret with a mysterious smile. "You may have noticed that I referred to him as a shepherd."

I nodded, curious.

Margaret leaned in close, her voice just barely above a whisper and said, "Jennifer, that wasn't an angel . . . it was *Jesus.* And *you* were one of the dear little sheep on his T-shirt."

She grinned as my mouth dropped open in surprise, then continued. "I told you earlier that your dreams reflect the character of God, who exists in the past, present, and future all at the same time. In this dream, Jesus was the one guiding and watching over you as you journeyed toward him on the mountain. He does not just wait for you to reach him. He is with you every

step of the way. And this is what your Shepherd calls to his
sheep:

> *"The past, present, and future are all tied together, dear
> one, and I watch with joy and excitement your journey
> toward me."*

Wow, I thought. More goose bumps. *I was one of his little
sheep. I would really like to have that T-shirt.*

Trinity

Long ago God spoke to our ancestors in many and various
ways by the prophets, but in these last days he has spoken
to us by a Son, whom he appointed heir of all things,
through whom he also created the worlds. He is the
reflection of God's glory and the exact imprint of God's very
being, and he sustains all things by his powerful word.

HEBREWS 1:1–3

Still marveling over the revelation that we are lovingly and joyfully shepherded through life by Jesus, I finally removed my 3-D
glasses. As I laid them on the table, several sharp barks interrupted my thoughts. All three dogs were huddled around the
back door, scratching and whining to be let inside. *How odd*, I
thought, *it is such a nice day outside.* The pups were quite insis-
tent, so I gathered up the 3-D glasses and hurried over to let
them into the house.

Stepping back out onto the porch, I sensed strangeness in the
air. It was still nice out, but there was an oppressive feeling that
hadn't been there a few minutes before. *Hmmm*, I thought. *Maybe
it is some atmospheric thing that dogs can sense and humans
cannot.* I walked back over to the garden to join Margaret, and as I

sat down in my chair, I was stunned to see that a miraculous change had taken place in my angel friend's appearance. Her entire being was radiating a glow of light, forming a halo all around her. The color of her gown had taken on a decidedly shimmering silver hue, and a huge silver shield now rested at her side against her chair. Light continued to radiate from her eyes, making those merry blues look somewhat fierce in their intensity. My sweet, funny Margaret was now appearing to me as the guardian in *guardian angel*!

She rose from her chair, and I noticed she had become significantly taller. I did not speak because I knew she was gearing up to say something important. I was too overwhelmed by what I was witnessing to say anything coherent anyway.

"Jennifer, in your life's journey with our Lord, you have learned a great deal about listening to him and that his messages may take time to understand. The Word of God speaks to us where we are, and he teaches us as we are ready to receive. And now our Father has deemed you ready for some messages of great importance."

Just as she finished speaking, a strong breeze suddenly picked its way through the tree branches above. Clouds began to swirl overhead in a darkening sky. The breeze increased until it was no longer a breeze but a steady wind picking up leaves and sending them skittering around the yard and across the patio. Startled birds took flight and went in search of the protection of a nest or secure tree branch. At first I thought this might be another approaching summer storm, but when I looked up at the dark clouds racing above our heads, I knew that was not the case. I had never seen anything like this. The air turned chilly, and I saw dark shapes flitting in and out of the swirling mass above. The sense of oppression grew heavy, and I began to feel afraid.

Margaret reached out and took my hand in hers. Immediately, the fear and sense of oppression I was experiencing vanished. And, oddly, Margaret and I were completely unaffected by the wind. It was as if we were enclosed in a safe cocoon. *Uh-oh*, I thought, *here comes another one of those serious heavenly angel moments!*

Her voice was now much louder and commanding. "Jennifer, I want you to stay seated so that you will remain within our protective cover," she instructed. *Our* protective cover? I covertly tried to peer around me, wondering if there was something or someone else I was not seeing but, of course, I saw nothing. Margaret continued. "The next two dreams we are going to explore were powerful and a bit frightening, wouldn't you agree?"

"Yes, they were," I answered, my heart beginning to pound.

Margaret leaned down slightly and looked directly at me, her intense blue eyes, now reflecting a steel-gray hue, penetrated mine. "Jenn, do you know what spiritual warfare is?"

"Um, I think so," I replied cautiously, dreading where this was going. This is a subject I didn't like to think about. "From what I've heard, I believe it is the constant battle being fought in the spiritual realm by God and his angels against Satan and his followers."

"You are quite correct, and that is why you are now seeing me as a warrior. Spiritual warfare was active while you were dreaming these next two dreams. God sent me and others much mightier than me to guard you while you dreamed and received his messages. Make no mistake, *the Enemy did not want you to remain in a dream state to receive God's message.* You needed help and we were there. Hear what the Word of God says: 'For he will command his angels concerning you to guard you in all your ways.'"

Gulp! That was a sobering thought. All I did was sleep and dream while the powers of light and darkness waged a war around me. It was frightening, but at the same time strangely comforting—yet I admit I was at that moment seriously considering purchasing a night light for use in the foreseeable future!

As if she could read my thoughts, Margaret laughed softly and said, "Don't be concerned. This happens all day long, every day, Jennifer. God is always watching over his children and fiercely defends those who bear his mark on their souls."

She picked up her shield and moved to stand behind me in my chair, placing her right hand on my shoulder. Her grip was so firm and determined that it hurt a little. "I will remain right here while you speak of your next two dreams . . . Let's begin."

The night is ink black as I run down the street to get back to my home. Others are doing the same, knowing full well that we are in great danger. Just as I leap into my house and slam the door closed, a tremendous, house-shaking roar fills the air, accompanied by a blinding bright light. Immediately there is a large explosion, and I hear screams of agony outside. I do not dare open my door be-

cause I have no idea when another of the harbingers of death will fall from the sky. It has been happening all night and I am exhausted. I want the morning to come so badly, because I know that with the dawn we will have a respite from the death and destruction until the following dusk, when it will all begin again. Some on the news are saying it is solar flares; others say the stars are falling. All I know is that they are points of light that fall indiscriminately from the sky and slam into the earth. Several more of these things fall throughout the night, and all I can hear are explosions and the agonized screams of people caught outside. I am aware that I am dreaming and I try to wake up, but it doesn't work, so I hide in a bathtub for the rest of the night. Finally, it falls quiet as the light of the morning sun fills the sky.

Breathing easier now that the new day has arrived, I get up and prepare myself to go outside and try to attend to anyone needing help. With some surprise, I notice that I am very pregnant. I move slowly down the road, stepping carefully so as not to trip on the large amount of debris and rubble. I do not see any people, injured or otherwise, so I assume they must have already been helped or have found shelter. It is so very quiet. All I can hear is gravel and broken glass crunching beneath my feet. Suddenly, I realize I am in labor and am going to give birth right here on the street. I deliver my baby in a hospital laundry cart. It is a little boy! I pull him up into my lap and am amazed at how big he is—he looks to be the size *of a two-year-old. He looks up at me with admiring big blue eyes, and then astonishingly he says, "Hello, Mother!" and smiles at me. We stand, he takes my hand, and we head back to the house together. It is mind-boggling that this naked, newborn child is so grown up, can walk and talk. He completely takes charge, as if he is the one taking care of me. I do not have a word to say, all I can do is smile at him.*

The day passes, apparently peacefully, because the next scene I remember is strolling down to the shore of a large, peaceful lake with my beautiful boy. He still wears no clothes, and he stands at the silvery water's edge, turning to look at me with his wonderful smile. I begin feeling anxious as I notice the sun is low in the orange sky behind him. With the setting of the sun, the terror from the skies will return. I call out to my child that it is time for us to go home. He stays where he is at the water's edge and says to me, "Mother, I have to go to my father now." "Your father?" I reply, mystified. I have no idea who this child's father is. "Yes, Mother," he replies, "my father is the sun." He turns away from me and points directly at the setting sun. With that, he begins to wade deeper into the water. "No! No! Child, don't go in the water, you will drown!" I cry out. My beautiful boy turns back to me and smiles. "Don't worry, Mother, I will be just fine. I am going to my father now, but I will always be near if you need me." He wades out into the calm silver water toward the setting sun and disappears. Strangely, his words have a great

calming effect on me, and I no longer worry about my
child. I turn and leave the lake behind me.

Time passes, and in the next scene, I am being swept
through the middle of town in a raging river. I, along with
many other people, am fighting to keep my head above
water as we are pushed along by the strong current. I can
see shops and docks along the riverbank and lots of debris
floating in the water with us, as if this is some kind of
flood. I look over the heads of several people and some-
thing catches my eye. I suck in my breath, absolutely
stunned. There, floating as calmly as can be in the water
across the river from me, is my little boy! He smiles his big
smile at me, and I can hear his voice as if he is whispering
right into my ear. He says, "Don't be afraid, Mother! You
see? I am always here!" The river becomes calm, and I lay
my head back in the water and just float, completely re-
laxed. I am no longer afraid. Finally, I awaken.

I swiveled in my chair to look up at Margaret. Without re-
moving her hand from my shoulder, she spoke. "This is a powerful dream our Lord has shared with you, my child—particularly
in its energy *and* imagery. I'd like to hear your immediate impressions of it."

"It was powerful," I agreed, "and when I woke up, I was exhausted. I experienced so many conflicting emotions associated
with the mysterious images in the dream—stars of terror raining
from the night sky, a pregnancy and birth, the setting sun, a
large peaceful lake, and a raging river. And the child. As I began

to think about the dream, I puzzled over the comment by the child that 'my father is the sun.' Then it hit me with a force that took my breath away. Not the sun, but the *Son*! I knew there was an important message buried deep inside this dream, but I really could not get my head around it enough to come up with any reasonable interpretations, so I laid it aside, trusting God would reveal its message when he felt I was ready. The only thing I knew for a fact was that the child in my dream was Jesus.

"And, okay, the laundry cart. I know exactly where this image came from. When I'd had this dream, I was working for a hospital system in Ohio and had recently been assigned an office in the basement of one of the hospitals in the laundry department. Some days I literally had to climb over mountains of bags of dirty hospital laundry in order to get into my office. Apparently, it caused enough stress to make its way into my dream."

Margaret laughed. "Yes, Jenn, things of your everyday world can very easily work themselves into your dreams! Let's move forward a few years now to when you had a surprising revelation about the events that take place in your dream."

I continued. "After Guy and I moved to Houston, I joined a disciple Bible study at a church near our home. While reading my homework toward the end of the thirty-four-week study, I turned my attention to Revelation chapter twelve. After reading a few verses, I had a funny sensation that I had seen this material before. Strange, since this was the first time I had read or studied the Book of Revelation. As I read further into the chapter, I realized something so startling that it downright frightened me. *This chapter was my dream!* I slammed my Bible shut and jumped up from the couch where I had been comfortably reading. I was actually trembling and had to walk away for a while to gather my wits about me and to muster up the courage to open my Bible again."

"That must have been quite a shock," said Margaret. "When God decides to reveal something, he certainly grabs your attention! Can you tell me briefly what this passage from Revelation said?"

"Sure," I answered. "I remember it pretty clearly. In the twelfth chapter of Revelation, a pregnant woman is in labor, and a dragon sweeps a third of the stars from heaven to earth with his tail. The woman gives birth to a male child, who is to rule all nations, but her child is caught up and taken to God and to his throne. The woman flees into the wilderness. She is protected and nourished there for three and a half years. Then a serpent pours a river of water out of his mouth after the woman, to sweep her away in a flood.

"Margaret, I was absolutely astounded that this scripture so closely matched the events in my dream. I have learned a lot about this passage by consulting other sources and understand its meaning pretty well as it relates to the scriptures, but I still am wondering what God's message was for *me* in all of this."

"I can help you with that," said Margaret. "Let's begin with your dream's images of the terrifying, exploding objects falling throughout the night—stars, you mentioned—and the quiet peace that the morning sun brought. Now consider the beginning part of the scripture you read about a dragon sweeping the stars from heaven with his tail. The dragon, Jenn, represents

Satan as he was cast out of heaven, along with his fallen angels. This being of Light was cast into Darkness, where he would live and reign, unleashing his havoc on earth and on the children of Light. The images in your dream—the night terror balanced by the morning peace—reflect the ongoing battle between the realms of Light and Darkness. In other words, the reality of spiritual warfare was being revealed to you."

Margaret paused, and a little shiver ran up my spine. "The battle is fierce," she acknowledged, noticing my reaction. "But the presence of the sun in your dream brings you the assurance that Light will always rule over Darkness. Are you with me so far?"

I nodded and she continued.

"You mentioned earlier that the one thing you knew for a fact was that the child in your dream was Jesus, and you are correct. God was doing something very special with the images he sent you of the child, the sun, and the 'woman' caught in the flooding, raging river. In this dream, God revealed himself to you as the Trinity—Father, Son, and Spirit. As the child said to you, *'my father is the sun,'* you correctly realized that he meant 'Son.' In this statement, God revealed the Divinity of Christ— that the father and the son are One.

"And, as you were carried along in the flooding river in your dream, you heard your child's voice whisper to you, 'Don't be afraid, Mother. You see? *I am always here!'* In this portion of your dream God revealed the third person of the Trinity—the Holy Spirit, the comforter and advocate, the One who is always with you, no matter what trials you face.

"Additionally, your role as the mother of the child in your dream correlates to the woman in the Revelation twelve scripture, who is considered to be the heavenly representative of God's people—the nation of Israel and the Christian Church. As the child gently whispered his words of comfort to his mother in the river in your dream, think about what a deep expression of God's love this was, not only for you personally, but also for Israel and for his Church!"

I sat, spellbound. I never could have come up with these profound revelations on my own. I thought about what Margaret had told me and then shared a few of my own thoughts with her.

"As scary as it is, I have to admit I do believe spiritual warfare is real, Margaret. The chaos, hatred, and violence in this world seem only to be getting worse. Thankfully, I know there is only one place in which my hope rests. I choose the Light, and I trust the Trinity."

"My dear girl, you have no idea how much your words please the One in whom you place your trust," said Margaret, "and this is his response:

"Treasure of my heart, I have revealed myself to you as Father, Son, and Spirit, and I want you to know that I am here with you always. Do not fear the future and the trials it will bring. Because you believe in me, I am forever your deliverer. Hope and victory abide in me."

The Table Is Set

Behold, I send an angel before you to guard you on the way
and to bring you to the place that I have prepared. Pay
careful attention to him and obey his voice . . .

EXODUS 23:20–21

Margaret strengthened her already-firm hold on my shoulder, her grip like an anchor, keeping me in my chair. I was thankful for the protective cocoon she had built around us, for the winds had reached a howling pitch and the eerie black clouds continued to darken and swirl in the sky above. I swiveled in my chair again to peer up at Margaret, and I saw—*Oh, my goodness!*—*I saw two faint outlines appear on either side of her . . .* very tall, silver-robed male figures standing silently at attention.

"Whoa, Margaret!" I gasped, thoroughly shaken. "You brought *reinforcements*?" Even though the wind did not touch us, I still felt a chill go up my spine. Now I knew what she had meant earlier when she referred to me remaining "under *our* protective cover."

My wide-eyed expression obviously translated my thoughts because Margaret nodded and gave me a serious little smile.

"They are mighty warriors, dear child, but do not be afraid. They were part of this next dream. At the command of the Holy One, they were there to provide assistance and guidance to you."

I looked up at these mighty angels, and as I did, they both slowly nodded their heads in confirmation of Margaret's words.

"Continue with your next dream, Jenn," said Margaret, "and take comfort in our presence."

I am sitting in the back pew of the darkened nave, the main aisle of a Gothic-style cathedral constructed of dark gray stone. I face the altar, and before it is the transept, a rectangular area that cuts perpendicular across the main aisle and gives a cathedral the shape of a cross. A brilliant white light, flashing like lightning, is emanating from the arched entrance of the chamber on the left side of the transept, and I can hear screams and terrible explosions coming from the chamber. Three figures in dark hooded robes run from this terrifying chamber. Two of them cross the main aisle and disappear into the dark, yawning void of the transept chamber on the right. The third comes to a halt in the middle of the transept, the altar behind him. He turns, looks directly at me, raises his arm, and with a grossly gnarled finger points at me and hisses, "Don't you dare!" as if he is warning me not to come any nearer or to interfere. I am so frightened I feel as though I am going to faint, even though I am sitting down. The evil emanating from him is tangible. I want very badly to wake up, but something makes me stand up and move up the aisle in defiance of the hooded figure before me. This is in total opposition to my personality, which overwhelmingly prefers to avoid danger or confrontation. I am aware that what I really want to do is run the other way. The figure hisses again and then runs to join the other two. I continue after him, terrified, feeling as if I am being pushed from behind.

I enter the dark chamber and am immediately surrounded by the three hooded figures. As they tighten their circle around me, they growl and hiss and throw off their hoods. I am greatly dismayed to discover they are demons. They are horribly ugly, with thick green-and-yellow skin, and are intent on doing me great harm. I frantically try to think of ways to repel them, and the only thing that comes to mind is to recite the Twenty-Third Psalm. I begin to say it out loud, but only get through, "The Lord is my Shepherd, I shall not want. He makes me lie down in green pastures . . ." At this point, I cannot remember any of the words that follow. I begin trying to wake myself up, because I know I am dreaming and that if I do not wake up, these demons are going to get hold of me. Suddenly, there is a whisper in my ear. "Say the Lord's Prayer—you know this!"

So I begin to shout the words as the demons circle ever tighter around me. "Our Father, who art in heaven, hallowed be thy name! Thy kingdom come, thy will be done, on earth as it is in heaven!" Suddenly, with the words "thy will be done, on earth as it is in heaven," the demons stop their advance on me as if repelled by an invisible force field and completely change their appearance. The demons are gone, but instead, standing around me are three young adult men who appear to be of Middle Eastern descent. They look at me with shocked, confused, terrified expressions, and then run away from me deeper into the chamber. They are gone!

Feeling safe at last, I leave this chamber and go back to see what is going on in the brilliantly lit chamber on the left side of the aisle. As I approach the archway, I notice that the screams and sounds of explosions have stopped. It is eerily quiet. Also, the formerly brilliant white light is now very subdued and has a reddish cast to it. I enter the chamber and am dismayed by what I see. There are huge mounds of broken concrete and twisted steel everywhere. Clouds of smoke drift in the air. I do not see any people. As I slowly negotiate my way through the rubble, I realize I am not alone. Two very tall figures are walking by my side, as if escorting me. All I can see is their robes, silently sweeping the ground as they move along. I sense a quiet peace and reverence from them. Something catches my eye and I discover that I have come across a Bible, almost hidden in the debris. I pick it up and dust it off. As I look farther ahead, I also spy a small red book. I walk over to pick it up as well. It is a Quran. I dust it off and carry it along with the Bible. Farther on, I see something blue and gold half buried by a huge chunk of concrete. We carefully climb over to it and I pull it from the rubble. It is ac-

tually two items, a blue book with gold scrollwork on the front, and a type of stole that is also blue and has gold scrollwork matching the book. A sense tells me it is a copy of the Hebrew Torah and a vestment. I add these to the other two books I have found. Suddenly, up ahead in the midst of the debris, a small round table appears, covered with a white linen tablecloth. I think that it curiously resembles some kind of altar. I am led to this table by my quiet escorts. There I lay all the items I have retrieved from the rubble. The three of us stand there silently, waiting. Then from up above, way above us, comes a loud voice that is so incredibly sad that it cuts like a sword to the very depths of my soul. The voice says, "The demons are killing my children!" With that, I am released and finally awaken.

My eyes were squeezed tightly closed as I finished the telling of this dream. It still felt so real, after all these years. I felt Margaret give my shoulder a comforting pat, and I knew she understood. Then she spoke.

"This was an important dream, Jennifer, because it contained prophecy of an event that changed the world you live in. I would like to hear about the thoughts and feelings you experienced when this prophecy was fulfilled. You talk for a bit. I'll listen."

I exhaled a long, slow, breath and began. "This dream, Margaret, was perhaps the most shocking dream I have ever had. I had this dream in November 2000, just before the Christmas holidays.

My first recollection upon awakening was the knowledge that the voice I heard was God, and that he was grieving terribly. For several days I experienced residual feelings of fear and dread and could not shake the profound sadness of the voice at the end of my dream. Although my heart told me I had received a really important communication from heaven, I had no idea what it meant. So, I just left it up to God to reveal his message when he was ready. And oh, my, Margaret, he *did* reveal the meaning of my dream nearly one year later—in a big, and terrible, way.

"On the morning of September 11, 2001, I watched in horror along with the rest of the country as terrorists slammed their planes into the World Trade Center towers in New York City and the Pentagon in Washington, D.C. Thousands of innocent people were killed, and we later learned about the Islamic fundamentalist organization, Al Qaeda, that claimed responsibility for this horrific event.

"As I watched the damaged towers slowly fall into a heap of twisted steel, concrete rubble, and smoke, my dream returned to me with the force of a whirlwind, constricting my heart and stomach so much that I could barely breathe. "Oh my Father," I wailed in stunned disbelief, "*this* is what you were showing me!" Needing to be with other believers, I called my church and learned they were already planning a special service that evening for people to come to mourn and to pray. I attended the service and wept with others as we prayed for those lost and for strength and guidance for our country. It was then that I began to understand the inconsolable grief I heard in my Father's voice in my dream."

"That was a terrible day, Jenn, for all of you and for us in heaven," affirmed Margaret. "Many prayers from the Kingdom covered the earth that day. Please, continue with your thoughts."

I kept going. "In the days following the tragedy, I watched as our nation and world came together in grief and prayer. A memorial service was held at Ground Zero. Representatives from Christianity, Judaism, and Islam were present together on the stage. As I watched the ceremony, listening to the heartfelt prayers for healing, my thoughts kept returning to the altar table in my dream where I laid the Christian Bible, the Islamic Quran, and the Hebrew Torah. And the voice, exclaiming with infinite sadness, 'The demons are killing my children!'

"As I considered the meaning of these images, the still, small voice inside me suddenly said 'children' and 'mercy.' I took this to mean there is a tremendous need for healing to occur between the peoples represented by the books I placed on the table, and more important, healing in their relationship with God."

"That was a wise assumption," said Margaret. "God created human beings to be in relationship with him, and this relationship is a free-will choice each person must make. This is a crucial choice. With whom will you choose to be aligned—the God of Light or the Prince of Darkness? As the September eleventh tragedy and subsequent world events have demonstrated, a great number of people have chosen Darkness, resulting in the shedding of precious human blood, and, as you have experienced in your dream, this grieves God terribly.

"Now, child, let's begin to look at the elements of your dream. Let's start with the two chambers in the cathedral—one full of light and the other a dark void. What do you think that means?"

Immediately, I thought of our previous conversation. "Would that be another reminder about the ever-present war between the spiritual realms of Light and Darkness?"

"Good girl!" said Margaret. "You were paying attention. Now, consider your position as you sat in the back of the cathedral, watching the drama unfolding between the chambers. You were perfectly happy to just sit and watch, until you felt an unseen force prompt you to pursue the demon. Your unwillingness to take part in what was going on represented complacency, Jenn, an unfortunate trait of human nature. It is much easier to ignore the atrocities going on around you than to get involved. The unseen force that you felt pushing you up the aisle was actually our two warrior angel friends here. *They knew that your active involvement as a believer was crucial to defeating the power Satan had over the events in your dream . . . and in the events of your daily life."*

Goose bumps, *again*. I felt a little ashamed about my own hesitance to get involved and had to admit that Margaret was right. It is much easier to say "There isn't anything I can do about it," than to take action. I privately decided I needed to work on that.

"Okay," Margaret continued, saving me from any more guilty feelings. "I want to look at two more elements of your dream . . . the Lord's Prayer and the Twenty-Third Psalm . . ."

"Oh, that was so strange, Margaret," I broke in. " For some weird reason I tried to say the Twenty-Third Psalm when I was so frightened by the demons. I would never think to do that if I was awake."

"We'll get to that in a minute, dear," continued Margaret. "Let's first talk about what happened when you said the Lord's Prayer in your dream."

"Well," I said, "I am guessing that it was my warrior angels who urged me to say the Lord's Prayer when I couldn't remember the psalm, is that right?" I waited for an answer and got a small, affirming squeeze on my shoulder. I continued. "I actually didn't get to say the whole prayer, because when I got to the part *'thy will be done, on earth as it is in heaven',* everything changed and the demons went away. That was pretty awesome."

"It *was* awesome, Jenn. These holy words broke the spell the power of Darkness had over those young men, freeing them. This is a powerful message. To establish the will of God on earth is one of the most important things human beings can do for themselves, because in doing so, the power of the Enemy is broken, allowing healing and restoration to occur. It is the Divine will of the Father that *all* of his beloved are restored to him."

I nodded slowly as I listened to this insight. This amazing angel was helping me see so much deeper into the meaning of this dream.

"*Now*, dear girl," Margaret continued. "Let's talk about the Twenty-Third Psalm. God had a specific reason for placing this into your dream, and the answer is buried in the words of the psalm itself. Listen carefully to verse five: '*You prepare a table before me in the presence of my enemies. You anoint my head with oil; my cup overflows.*'"

I sat, stunned, as Margaret let this sink in. Images from my dream flashed before my eyes . . . the demons, the altar table, the books . . .

"Oh, Margaret," I asked breathlessly, "God was trying to tell me something important about that altar table, wasn't he?"

"Yes, he was, child," answered Margaret, "and it's a message you were very close to understanding on your own. A few minutes ago, you mentioned you assumed the three books placed on the table in your dream represented people, and that there was a need for healing in their relationships with one another and with God. Those books *did* represent people, Jenn . . . not just peoples of the faiths represented by the three books, but *all* people. *God set his table with the cup of salvation, and invites all children to join him there—to soak in his anointing of love, healing, forgiveness, mercy, and grace.* Isn't that beautiful? God offers this table because he is not only a God of judgment. He is a God of grace. In his unfathomable mercy, he provides a way for those lost to Darkness to be restored to him. And that *way* is Jesus, the ever-present, overflowing cup of salvation. Do you remember Jesus' message for you when we discussed your personal encounter with him? *'No darkness is too dark, no circumstance is too dire for me to walk into with my Light and free you.'* What a comforting message that is for a world suffering from violence and terror."

"Wow, Margaret," I said. "That is beautifully said, and is a lot to absorb!"

"I'm going to give you a little bit more to absorb, dear, because there is a serious *warning* about God's table. If you remove yourselves from the table because of hatred and violence toward one another, you fall prey to Satan and the power of Darkness. God grieves terribly about the destruction and death unleashed by his enemy, and his judgment will be fierce upon those who insist on remaining under Satan's power."

Yep, that's a serious warning, all right, I thought.

"There is so much more to this dream than I realized, Margaret," I said, "and it seems to keep revealing new truths over the years. I had a mind-blowing revelation about this dream *ten years* after the September eleventh attack."

"Oh?" said Margaret mysteriously. "Tell me."

"Well," I replied, "this revelation occurred on September 10, 2011—just one day shy of the tenth anniversary of the 9/11 tragedy. I was once again in Maine and took the local newspaper down to the beach to read about the preparations for the next day's memorial ceremonies. I turned to the religion section and was stunned by the photograph printed on the first page. It was a picture of an open Bible fused into metal, found by a New York firefighter in the rubble of the fallen Twin Towers of the World Trade Center.

"I was so overcome by what I saw in front of me. I had always considered the Bible and other books found in the rubble to be important *symbols* in my dream. But what God showed me that day on the beach was that the Bible in my dream wasn't just a symbol. *It was real.* There in front of me, printed in the newspaper, was a photograph of a Bible, fused in a heart-shaped shard of metal actually found in the rubble. And I'll bet that heart shape meant that God loves us—like a little love note from him. That just amazed me, Margaret!"

"Did you bother to look to see what the scripture said on the exposed pages of that Bible?" Margaret asked,

"Uh, no," I replied. "I didn't think to do that. Why?"

Margaret laughed softly. "If you had looked closely, Jennifer, you would have seen that *God left a message for humanity in the aftermath of the terror attack.* The Bible was open to Matthew chapter five, where Jesus gave his famous Sermon on the Mount. This page contains Jesus' teaching on the Law of Retaliation, and the Law of Love. He states: *'You have heard that it was said "You shall love your neighbor and hate your enemy." But I say to you, Love your enemies and pray for those who persecute you, so that you may be sons of your Father who is in heaven. For he makes his sun rise on the evil and the good, and sends rain on the just and the unjust.'*

"This is a clear message to extend the love and mercy of God to those who are the most difficult to love. You have a responsibility to pray for those who hurt you and for those who have become lost in the Darkness, so that their hearts might be changed and that they will repent and accept the mercy and salvation so freely offered. This is a very difficult concept for humanity to grasp, but it is of utmost importance. The truth as Jesus spoke it two thousand years ago remains truth today. You mentioned, Jenn, that your dream keeps revealing truth, and you are right. Prophecy speaks through the ages."

Okay. I was blown away again. "Margaret, you have taught me so much that my head is spinning," I said. "I have a much clearer picture of what God was teaching me in this dream. It is imperative that we no longer 'sit in the back of the cathedral,' watching and doing nothing about the events going on in our world. As children of God and heirs to his Kingdom, we need to come together and be prayerfully active to bring his love and mercy to all peoples of the world. By doing so, the power of his love will destroy the hold that the Enemy has over our lives. *Thy will be done, on earth as it is in heaven."*

"I am proud of you, Jennifer." Margaret said fondly. "And I love how your heart pursues and embraces the revelations God sends you in your dreams. As we leave our discussion of this prophetic dream, hear God's whisper of invitation to you:

"I have prepared a special place for you at my table, precious one, where you and any you invite can rest in my eternal promise of mercy, love, and salvation. Beware of embracing hatred, because it will remove you from my table and from my protection. That, my love, would cause me unbearable sorrow."

Oh. Those beautiful words nearly broke my heart.

Rainbows and Roses

Don't let your hearts be troubled. Trust in God, and trust
also in me. There is more than enough room in my Father's
home. If this were not so, would I have told you that I am
going to prepare a place for you? When everything is ready,
I will come and get you, so that you will always be with me
where I am.

JOHN 14:1–3

And this is the promise that he made to us—eternal life.

1 JOHN 2:25

I tilted my head back and exhaled a long, slow breath. The telling of these past two dreams had been both exhausting and ex-
hilarating. Margaret's firm grip, still on my shoulder, softened as
she gave me a gentle pat. The wind slowly wound down to a
pleasant breeze, and the turbulence overhead parted and melted
away to reveal a deep-blue sky dotted with white, puffy clouds.

Looking up at Margaret, I noticed more changes taking
place in her appearance, as well as that of our two silent friends.
Margaret's gown had turned from silver to a sparkling mix of sky
blue and green, reflecting perfectly the sky and the treetops
swaying in the breeze. Her shield was gone. Our other two com-

panions were also transforming before my eyes. Their silver robes were now white as snow, glowing faintly as if lit from within. Their faces were shining so brightly that I could not quite make out their features. They both nodded at me, and I instinctively knew they were smiling.

"Our friends are soon going to return to their home with our Father," said Margaret softly, "but first they wish to stroll about and enjoy your beautiful gardens." With a mysterious twinkle in her eye, she leaned in close and whispered in my ear, "Watch them closely as they depart!"

My heart was filled with love and gratitude for these two mighty, gentle beings because I now knew that they, along with Margaret, had been the angels watching over me during my dreams. They helped me to remain asleep in order to dream and receive the messages my Lord had intended for me. They gently prodded and guided me down the aisle after the demon's challenge and prompted me in my confusion and terror to say the Lord's Prayer in order to break Satan's power. They were my quiet escorts as I picked the three books from the rubble and placed them on the altar table.

My eyes filled with tears as I thanked them. "You were there for me, and I cannot even begin to tell you how much that means to me. It is so comforting—and empowering—to know that you are there fighting for me even when I cannot see you. Our God is a mighty and wonderful God to provide the protection of his angels for the children he loves so much! I hope I will see you again someday. Until then, thank you with all my heart. God bless you."

The large angels nodded at me in unison once more and moved slowly out into the yard. As they brushed silently by me, I caught a whiff of the unmistakable scent of white roses.

Margaret and I stood and watched our companions slowly roam about the gardens, stopping to observe a monarch butterfly immerse itself in the deep-purple blooms of a butterfly bush. In the hummingbird garden, they watched as a ruby-throated hummingbird zipped in and paused to sip sweet nectar from a sparkling red-glass feeder. They wandered over to the statue of St. Francis of Assisi, and as they did so, one of our resident bluebirds swooped down to take a drink of water from the basket in the statue's arms. Finally, as they walked through the back of the yard toward a large boulder hewn from the rocky hills of northwest Texas, the most magical thing happened.

The angels began to disappear, but it seemed as if they were moving through a strange doorway. A shaft of light, like a vertical slit, appeared, and immediately formed a brilliant rainbow prism that fanned out on both sides as they walked through. My breath caught in my throat as I realized the intense colors in the prism were the familiar colors of the rainbow, *but also included colors I had never seen before!* I passed my hand before my eyes, because I really could not believe what I was seeing. The colors were still there, and as the angels passed through this entryway, the prism folded around them, shrunk to a sliver of blinding bright light, and then disappeared altogether. The bluebird that had been drinking from the St. Francis statue flew right through the space the angels had just departed from and landed on top of his birdhouse in the back of the yard.

"Oh, Margaret," I breathed, "how absolutely *beautiful*. The doorway to heaven cracked open for barely a second and the light just spilled out! I had no idea there were so many colors."

"That was a special gift our friends left with you, my child," said Margaret.

I stood there in amazement as I absorbed what I had just witnessed, and a thought occurred to me. "When I'm watering my gardens and the water spray hits the sunlight just right, a rainbow appears out of nowhere. I have often marveled that those rainbows are probably always there, but just need the right conditions to occur in order for them to be revealed.

"But—wow—what happened just now tells me that heaven is like the rainbows. God and our two angel friends just now chose to give me a brief, beautiful peek at a realm unseen by human eyes."

"I have an idea," said Margaret in a whisper. "Let's go over to the spot where they left. Come!" Motioning to the back of the yard by the bluebird house, she picked up the hem of her gown and began hurrying through the cool grass. I joined her, and as we reached the spot where the prism of colors and shaft of light had briefly existed, I caught a slight lingering scent of the white roses. There was nothing left to see but my yard, just as it always had been.

Margaret stretched out her arms and began twirling slowly around. "Do this, too," she challenged. So I stretched my arms wide and began twirling very slowly, secretly hoping that no neighbors would choose to pick this particular moment to look out their window into my yard!

"Now, Jenn, think about this as you gently cut through the air around you with your arms. Heaven is all around us, although with your earthly eyes you cannot see it. So right now, even as you are circling around in your backyard with your arms outstretched, you are embracing heaven."

My heart began to beat a little faster as I tried to grasp the concept of embracing heaven. Oh, how I wished I could reach out with my wide-open arms and give Jesus a great big hug. I lifted my face toward the warm sun, closed my eyes, and kept twirling. When I began to get a little dizzy, I stopped and opened my eyes. Margaret had already stopped twirling and was watching me with a look of pure joy. I could sense another important message coming my way.

"Dear child," said Margaret, her voice just above a whisper, "heaven has always been a great mystery here on earth. I know you have been given a few precious glimpses into some truths about heaven, and I want you to tell me about them in a little while. But for now, our angel friends gave you this parting gift for a reason. Our Father wants you to know that the glimpses and little moments of truth that you have received about heaven are real and are from him. He encourages you to share what he has permitted you to see. He knows it will bring peace to those who have eyes that are open to see, a mind willing to accept, a heart tuned to the Word of God, and arms prepared to embrace joys that cannot even be imagined."

Margaret suddenly began fanning herself with her hands, making her soft white hair dance in wisps around her face. "Whew! My goodness, it is really getting warm out here. Let's get something cool to drink and return to our spot by the garden. Then we can speak more of heaven."

I left Margaret sitting out under the umbrella as I went inside to fetch some tall glasses of ice-cold water. "Welcome to warm and humid Texas, Margaret," I teased, as I set our frosty glasses on the table. "It has taken a while to get used to, but now I love it, especially how the air feels lazy and soft."

"Mm." Margaret nodded as she sipped her cool drink. Large beads of condensation trickled off the end of her glass and plopped onto her gown. They went unnoticed as she peered intently through the gardenia bushes planted in the garden next to us.

"Jenn, what is that sweet little plaque resting against the bottom of one of the columns?" she asked.

"Oh," I sighed wistfully, "that is a memorial for my little dog, named Mia. Several years ago at our former home, Mia escaped from our yard, became lost, and while trying to find her way back, she was hit by a car and killed. We found her in the road and brought her home to bury her in our garden. It completely shattered our hearts. We loved her so very much. She always liked to roam about the yard, sniffing the flowers, so I thought it would be nice to put a memorial here in this garden . . . to keep a part of her with us. I call this 'Mia's garden.'"

I paused as I felt the sadness of this memory tug on my heart.

"I'm so sorry, Jennifer," Margaret said gently. "I know how difficult losing Mia was for you. Something special happened the day after she died . . . do you remember?"

"Yes, I do remember. A remarkable encounter—I have always wondered about it."

"Tell me," Margaret prompted.

"Well, Guy and I were so devastated by Mia's sudden death that we hardly knew how to function. The day after she died, we decided we had to get out of the house and go do something, so we put our other little dog, Isabel, in the car and we drove down to Galveston Island, our favorite place to take the dogs for long walks on the beach. I cried my heart out as we wandered along the beach, thinking about how much I missed my little Mia. Finally the tears subsided, and we took some comfort in watching Isabel happily chase after little sandpipers near the water's edge.

"We came upon two men who stopped us and asked us about Isabel. They asked if she was an Italian greyhound, to which we answered yes. They went on to say that one of them had had an Italian greyhound that had been hit by a car and killed, and how difficult that time had been for him. I was stunned. We had not even mentioned our Mia, that she was also an Italian greyhound and had been struck and killed by a car just the day before. As we talked with the two men about Mia and our similar circumstance, I felt calmed by their words, and for the first time since Mia's death, felt peace begin to creep into my heart. After a while they said their good-byes and walked away from us. We never saw them again."

"What struck you as so remarkable about this encounter?" asked Margaret.

"The conversation we had with those two men was so specific to our situation," I answered. "Usually, when people saw our dogs, they said things like, 'Cute dogs . . . what kind are they?' and moved on. Something has always told me that meeting those men really wasn't a coincidence. It wasn't, was it, Margaret?"

"Specific encounters like what you just described are never coincidences, child," said Margaret softly. "Your instinct was correct. Those 'men' you met were angels, sent by God to heal the broken hearts of two of his children that day on the beach. This was another heavenly intersection along your life's path."

Margaret paused to let me absorb this truth for a moment and then asked, "Do you believe Mia is in heaven?"

"Oh, yes, Margaret, I absolutely do," I answered without hesitation. "My pets are such an important part of my life. They have always provided me with unconditional love and comfort, characteristics of the Creator himself. I have no doubt God sent them to me and that, when they die, he takes them home to wait for that happy day when we will all be reunited."

"Our God is such a good and loving God," nodded Margaret, her eyes misting with tears. "Your little Mia and all your other beloved pets are in his benevolent hands."

"I know you are speaking the truth," I said with a tender smile. "I think of my sweet dogs and cats romping and playing together in heaven, in fields of green grass sprinkled with wildflowers and alive with butterflies. Cool shade trees line the bank of a nearby stream of clear, cold water, where they can rest and drink. That little 'mind picture' gives me great comfort and always makes me smile.

"I love to hear what other people's 'mind pictures' of heaven are like," I continued. "When I was little, I thought heaven was a bunch of white clouds that you drifted on while playing the harp. It actually seemed pretty boring, except for the playing the harp part. One of my childhood friends told me that heaven looked like a gingerbread house—no . . . a gingerbread *city*—on steroids. It had buildings made of pearls, rubies, emeralds, and silver, streets made of gold and diamonds, and everything sparkled in a brilliant light.

"I have also heard heaven described as sitting in a beautiful garden with Jesus, an eternal church service, and a mysterious misty-looking place where spirits just kind of drift around."

At the mention of the drifting spirits, I heard another unangel-like sound erupt from Margaret. She had her hands clapped over her mouth, but I could tell she was beaming from ear to ear. "That's a funny one!" she giggled.

"Well, I am relieved you think it funny, Margaret," I said, "because that means it is not so. Heaven is a very mysterious place to us humans, you know."

"Yes, I do know," said Margaret, "and as one who resides in heaven, I am greatly enjoying this conversation. Tell me some more impressions you have heard."

I thought for a second, and then a bright smile lit my face as I recalled a precious memory of my mother's. "My mother recently told me that when she was a girl, she'd thought that when it was your time to die, a huge platform would be lowered from the sky by big ropes. You would jump on the platform and then be raised up into heaven."

"Oh, how darling. I love that!" exclaimed Margaret, clapping her hands. "Her description reminds me of a giant swing."

I nodded, smiling. "I like that one, too. So, Margaret, *you* live in heaven. Can you tell me what it is *really* like?"

"I was wondering when you were going to ask me that," she laughed. "There are no human words to accurately describe heaven, child. I can assure you, it is a marvelous place—beyond marvelous, actually. One day you will see it for yourself with new eyes, and you will be overjoyed. But, I am not permitted to tell you anything more than that. I can only help you understand the little glimpses our Father has shared with you."

"I think I'll stick with the glimpses for now," I quipped. "I'm not in that much of a hurry to find out for myself!"

That drew a hearty laugh from Margaret.

"Okay, now, dear girl," Margaret encouraged with a glimmer in her eye, "tell me about your grandfather."

My face must have registered my shock, because Margaret laughed. "I can't believe you know about that!" I gasped. "I keep forgetting you are an angel . . . of course you know. My very first, really serious glimpses into heaven came from my beloved Granddaddy Gordon, my father's father.

"Granddaddy Gordon and I had a very special relationship. We loved being together. We took walks, worked in the garden, and we talked about lots of things. He always told me he was proud of me, and that meant so much to a young lady who was very naive and needed improvement in her self-confidence. Granddaddy had a heart condition. If I remember correctly, he had what was called hardening of the arteries. He experienced several heart attacks before he died. Ten years before he died, he suffered a heart attack, but that time an amazing thing happened to him. He said when he had this episode, he was taken to a beautiful garden. He was standing at one end of a footbridge that crossed over a gently running stream. At the other end of the footbridge was a beautiful woman, dressed in white. She called him by his name—'Gordon!'—and told him he must not cross over the bridge to her because his time on earth was not finished. He so very much wanted to cross the bridge, but was firmly told no.

"From then on, Granddaddy told this story and talked fondly about 'his angel.' This was really big to me, because by that time I was nurturing a deep, personal relationship with Christ, and I had often wondered where my beloved granddaddy stood with regard to God. He was raised in church, but something happened later in his life to turn him away. Thankfully, the loving influence of his second wife, Myrtle, led him back to his faith. It touched my heart to hear him talk openly about his angel. I thought it was wonderful that God would nurture his beloved Gordon's renewed faith through a planned encounter with one of his angels.

"Ten years later, Granddaddy Gordon finally got to cross the bridge in the beautiful garden and returned home to his Lord. I was devastated, yet thankful for his presence in my life and that he was now home with my beloved Jesus. The one thing I did not expect was that my relationship with Granddaddy wasn't over. He had a very special gift of love to give me after he died. When we arrived at the funeral home for visiting hours the day before the funeral, I went up to the casket to see him. This is *not* my favorite thing to do, but my heart was broken, and I loved him so much that I wanted to see him one more time. When I looked at him, I was really taken by surprise. The man in the casket was not my beloved granddaddy. He looked like him, yes, but the essence, the person I knew and loved, was not there. This was the first moment in my life when I realized, unequivocally, that *there is a soul*, and that when someone dies it leaves and goes to a better place. That was my granddaddy Gordon's final gift to me. It was poignant, personal, and eternal. In fact, to preserve that moment in my memory, I took a small yellow rose from the spray covering his casket and placed it in my Bible, so that whenever I came across it, it would remind me of his precious gift."

I paused a moment to take a sip of my water while it was still cool—the ice was melting quickly. As I placed my glass back down on the table, I noticed Margaret was holding something in her hands. It looked—why . . . it looked like a yellow rose!

My dear angel friend reached out and placed the delicate yellow rose in my hand, folding my fingers gently around the stem with her own. I waited for the prick of the thorns and then realized that there weren't any. Margaret held my hand in hers and said softly, "This, Jenn, is a special rose, because it is from heaven. Take it and put it in your garden, and tend to it carefully, for it will grow and flourish. I want you to have something alive and beautiful to remember your special grandfather, for *just as the rose is, he is*."

Her last words flooded my heart with comfort. I brought the rose to my face and inhaled its wonderful fragrance; it was like nothing I have ever experienced before. I had a big lump in my throat and it was hard to get any words out, but I managed to nod and say "Thank you" as I buried my face in the rose again to whisper a quick prayer of thanks to my Father in heaven for this marvelous and precious gift. Then I carefully placed the rose in my water glass to sustain it until I had a chance to plant it.

When I regained control of my voice, I continued with my story about Granddaddy. "Granddaddy's story still doesn't end, Margaret. God has given me a spiritual gift that I cannot put a name to, and I know of many others who have experienced this same thing. Occasionally, while I sleep, I have experienced what I call visits from Granddaddy Gordon and several others close to me who have died. When I see him, I walk and talk with him. We are always so happy to see each other, and he looks younger than I ever remember him. He seems to just 'check in' every once in a while.

"Another special visit was from a dear friend, Ed, whom I met while working as a volunteer at a local hospital. Ed was seventy-three years old, and we were assigned to deliver lunches and flowers to new mothers. We became instant friends and shared many wonderful conversations. Ed had undergone extensive chemo treatments for cancer the year before we met and was in remission. But, sadly, the cancer returned with a vengeance. At the end of his life, he was also diagnosed with ALS, Lou Gehrig's disease. It seemed particularly harsh for him to be suffering from two dreadful diseases at the same time. Though I only knew Ed for a brief period of my life, he held a very special place in my heart. Several months after his death, I had a dream visit from Ed. He was bathed in a beautiful blue light and looked so well and happy. He smiled at me and said, 'They are working again, Jennifer!' and he wiggled his legs. In my dream I was confused and did not understand what he meant. Nevertheless we continued to talk, and then Ed told me that now that he had let me know he was okay, I would not hear from him anymore, and true to his word, I haven't. When I woke up, I thought about our conversation, and then the realization struck me that Ed had been referring to regaining the use of his legs, which he had lost shortly before he died. Greatly comforted, I was able to let my friend go, knowing he was renewed and happy.

"What I also realized was that during these and other dream visits I have experienced, there is an unmistakable sense of excitement in the air. As if those I am visiting with are waiting, in anticipation of something."

"What do you think they are waiting for?" asked Margaret.

"I confess, I don't know. Seeing their loved ones again, maybe?" I guessed.

"You are very close," said Margaret. "They are waiting for the return of Christ, when all will be reunited with him in his eternal Kingdom. When you see and experience the anticipation of those you have had visits from, be encouraged that those gone before you know there is something infinitely more wondrous to come!"

A flutter of excitement began in my heart and quickly spread throughout my whole being. I could only imagine the wonders awaiting us.

"Margaret, this has been an amazing day. Today I witnessed a dazzling display of color and light as our angel friends returned to heaven, and then I received this precious rose as a gift to remind me that Granddaddy lives in heaven. Both are startling in their testimony that the realm of heaven is present, active, and vibrant—as vibrant as those magnificent, breathtaking colors."

"God has shared some precious glimpses of heaven with you, my child," Margaret agreed, her amusement evident in those twinkling blue eyes. "And let me leave you with a thought about those breathtaking colors. The next time you see a rainbow in the sky, picture in your mind God cracking the door of heaven open, just a wee bit, to look down and say 'I love you.' And as he cracks the door open, like he did today in your backyard, some of those magnificent colors spill out, forming the rainbow. God said to Noah regarding his rainbow, 'This is the sign of the covenant that I have established between me and all flesh that is on the earth.' So every once in a while, our Father delights his earthly children by sending the rainbow as a reminder of his love, his promise and his presence."

"Now, *that* is the most beautiful description of a rainbow I have ever heard." My mind whirled with images of rainbows I have seen, and one in particular jumped out at me. "Hey! Guess what? I even have rainbows in my *hair*!"

My angel laughed her soft, musical laugh and nodded. "And?" she prompted.

"When I am out in the sun, sometimes the wind blows my hair into my face and around my eyes. The strands nearest my eyes become magnified, and I can see teeny, tiny rainbows dance up and down the strands of my hair. That has always intrigued me."

"It is no surprise to me, sweet girl," said Margaret matter-of-factly. "You have the very DNA of God in you because you are his child. *Of course* you have rainbows in your hair!"

I sat in amazement of that revelation and a smile slowly crept across my face. Margaret finally stood and stretched. "It is time for me to return to that beautiful place I, and many that you love, call home. Go happily about your day, Jenn, and I will return this evening. Tonight I want you to share with me your dreams of death and heaven, for they contain powerful revelations. I guarantee it will be a very special evening. Oh, and keep your ears open, because I think God has a special message to share with his rainbow girl."

Before I could even manage a word of good-bye, Margaret faded into the sunlight; her blue-and-green gown shimmered and merged with the blues and greens of the sky and trees around us. Her familiar scent of white roses lingered behind.

I looked down at the table and the glass containing the single yellow rose. Remembering Margaret's instructions, I found a perfect spot in my garden and planted the rose, thanking God again for this special living gift to remind me of my granddaddy's life in heaven. I asked him to nurture and protect it, and to grow it someday into a beautiful rosebush.

As I dug in the soft, sandy soil, I suddenly heard a faint whispered response to my prayer:

"I love to send you glimpses of your future, sweet child of mine. Your days on earth are but an instant compared to the joyful existence that awaits you in my forever King-

dom. P.S.: I felt your embrace as you twirled in your backyard this morning. Thank you."

A surprised laugh escaped from me at those last words. Shaking my head in utter amazement, I stood, brushed the dirt off my knees, and went inside to tackle the growing pile of laundry that had been waiting ever so patiently for my attention.

Death and Life

And the dust returns to the ground it came from, and the
spirit returns to God who gave it.

ECCLESIASTES 12:7

Jesus answered him, "Truly I tell you, today you will be with
Me in paradise."

LUKE 23:43

A chorus of tree frogs began singing their evening vespers as I went out to the garden to await Margaret's return. The air was considerably more pleasant now, and a soft breeze gently tickled my wind chimes. Shadows crept across the yard as birds scouted the last few bites of food before returning to the comfort and safety of their nests for the night.

As I stood looking out at the backyard, my gaze fell upon the yellow rose I had planted earlier in the day. I did a double-take as a slight gasp escaped my lips. I had planted a single yellow rose, but there in its place was a small yellow *rosebush*! I shook my head slowly, smiling. God never failed to astound me with his glory and grace. Margaret was right. He so loves to surprise his children with gifts of love.

A soft, musical laugh interrupted my thoughts, and I looked over to the chairs by the garden to see Margaret standing there. She was an ethereal vision of light. Her gown was a soft white, shimmering with a radiance that cast a faint glow all around her body. I sensed that she had just come from the presence of the Holy Father himself and was still reflecting his glory.

"I see you followed my instructions, Jennifer," she said, her eyes sparkling with joy.

I rushed over to her and asked, "May I give you a hug?"

Without answering, Margaret reached out her arms and folded me into the most wonderful embrace. I leaned my head on her shoulder and just melted into the love and comfort that flowed out of her and into me.

After a few moments she released me and motioned for us to sit down in our chairs.

"When I left you earlier today," said Margaret, "we were beginning to discuss your insights about heaven. Your next revelations are nothing short of little miracles sent to you from the realm of the Almighty. So now, sweet daughter of God, I want you to tell me about your friend, Carol."

Carol. I sighed as a twinge of sadness tugged at my heart. "I met Carol in choir practice at my previous church. Actually, I sat next to her. More often than not she closed our rehearsals with a prayer, and she prayed so beautifully and from the heart, I could tell she had a very personal relationship with Jesus. I learned from others that five years earlier she had been diagnosed with and had undergone treatment for breast cancer, and was in complete remission. What a living testimony to God's healing and grace she was! Then one day, when it was time for our closing prayer, she asked if we would pray for her, because a routine cancer follow-up test was showing something that should not be there. As time went on, it became clear the cancer had returned and had spread.

"Carol amazed me with her grace, her bravery, and her joy in the midst of her battle with this terrible disease. She seemed to care more for our grief than she did for her own, and she continued to offer her beautiful prayers in choir practice, determined to keep singing. She sang with us for our Christmas and Easter cantatas. Then the cancer spread to her brain and walking became difficult as it affected her balance. She began using a wheelchair and was not able to come to choir practice, but did come to church with her beloved husband, Robert, whenever she felt up to it. One of her goals was to finish her treatments and be well enough to sing with us again at Christmas. Our hearts broken, we knew Carol's cancer was terminal, but we all prayed to keep her with us for as long as possible, and that she make her Christmas goal."

"Carol was an inspiration to all who met her," said Margaret tenderly, "and I believe you have learned that inspiration can come in rather surprising and mysterious forms, including your dreams. Would you share your dream about Carol with me now?"

I nodded in agreement as I began to tell my angel about a most extraordinary dream.

I am standing in a great hallway of an ornate, old building. High, arched windows run the length of the hallway

*on both sides, and smooth marble covers the walls and
floor. The building has a museum feel to it and reminds
me of photos I have seen of the New York Public Library.
There are lots of people moving about the hallway in both
directions, but no one I know. Then the crowd parts, and
I see Robert coming toward me, pushing Carol in her
wheelchair. She is wearing a short white hospital gown. It
looks as if she is "holding court" as people approach and
talk to her. I also approach Carol and, not knowing if she
can see or hear me, I say, "Carol, it is Jennifer." She replies,
"I know, and I am doing a little better." Then I am pushed
along in the crowd away from her. The hall suddenly becomes very quiet, and I realize that no one remains but
me, Robert, and Carol. Carol rises up out of her wheelchair and says, "I have to lie down awhile. I'm not feeling
very well." She stumbles over to a table I had not noticed
before. It reminds me of a sturdy, wooden physical ther-
apy table, and it is covered with a thick, deep cushion of
sheep's wool. Carol lies down on the table and buries her
face in the thick wool. As she settles into the wool, she
begins to moan and then begins to scream in agonizing
pain—soul-piercing, terrifying screams that make me so
frightened I cannot move. My heart wrenches and I feel
like I cannot breathe. I can only watch in horror, hopeful
that the deep, thick wool will bring comfort to her, and I
am thankful it is muffling her screams a bit. As I watch,
"others"—tall beings in white—appear and, along with
Robert, surround the table so completely that I can no*

*longer see Carol. Then the tall beings in white do a curi-
ous thing. They begin slowly and deliberately waving their
arms side to side above Carol, back and forth, back and
forth, as if they are somehow ministering to her. Carol's
screams become muffled and quieter. Finally, the scream-
ing stops altogether. The tall beings part and step back
from the table, and Carol raises herself up on her hands
and knees, crawls backward, and steps off the end of the
table. As soon as she stands up, three of the tall beings in
white surround her, linking their arms with hers. They
turn and move slowly down the hall away from me,
Robert, and the table. As she walks away, I notice that the
backs of Carol's legs are a fiery, angry red. I wonder to
myself if these red areas are where the pain has just left
her body. As Carol disappears with her escorts, I feel a
sense of relief—she is okay now. As I awaken, it is very
early in the morning. I lie quietly, shaken, very glad it was
"just a dream."*

I paused, remembering the intensity of this dream . . . it had
seemed so *real*.

"Jenn," Margaret said gently, bringing me back to our conversation. "Tell me what happened next."

"What happened next, Margaret, rocked my world. That
same day, early in the afternoon, I called the church office to col-
lect any prayer requests that had come in for the intercessory
prayer team, which I led. The church secretary told me that
"prayers are requested for Robert and his family because Carol

passed away early this morning." I was stunned. It was not expected to happen so soon, at least not by me. I could only groan with sadness. When I asked about what happened, the church secretary told me "Carol had a great day yesterday but last night she went downhill fast. According to her husband, she suffered incredible pain—it wasn't an easy way to go." She went on to say that Robert was home with her when she died.

"After hanging up the phone, I sat in my chair for a long time. Tears came as I mourned this beautiful sister in Christ. My heart was so sad, and I remember feeling frightened—just as I had been when I'd dreamed about my grandmother falling and breaking her back. What *was* this dream? It's as if I'd had a front row seat that in every sense permitted me to witness Carol's death. *Is that even possible?* And if it *was* possible, *why?*"

I looked to Margaret for an answer.

"I know this dream was distressing to you, Jennifer, but I want you to see it now for what it really was—a rare opportunity to witness the seamless transition from the earthly realm into the heavenly realm, and to understand that during this time of transition, you are never alone.

"Let's look at the images in your dream. Carol's family, friends, and husband, Robert, surrounded her while she was still living, and as she began the process of death, you saw 'tall beings in white' minister to her and eventually escort her away."

"Those tall beings were angels, weren't they?" I asked hopefully.

"Yes, child, they were," she answered. "They took away Carol's pain and escorted her Home."

"That's beautiful, Margaret," I said. Instead of feeling sadness, I suddenly felt like rejoicing for Carol.

Margaret smiled as she noticed the flicker of joy in my eyes. "Death, Jennifer, is not the *end* of life. Death is a *part* of life! In your dream, Carol did not cease to exist. On the contrary, after her earthly life ended on that table, she got up and continued on. God wanted you to see this important truth, dear one. You, and all his children, are spiritual beings having a human experience. When your human experience comes to an end, you return to your place of origin—behind the veil—into the waiting arms of the One who loves you like none other."

"Death is a *part* of life," I repeated thoughtfully. "Wow, I never thought about it quite that way. I can only imagine what it will be like to walk back into Jesus' arms like Carol did."

"There was something in your dream that gave you a clue about that. Remember the deep, thick cushion of sheep's wool that covered the table Carol lay on?"

Sheep's wool .... sheep ... Shepherd! "Oh, I *get* it, Margaret," I exclaimed. "It makes perfect sense. Jesus is the Lamb of God, the Great Comforter, the Great Physician, and our beloved Shepherd. Carol, during the process of dying, was able to rest in the arms of her beloved Jesus. My goodness, I can't think of anything more beautiful or comforting than that."

"And I can't think of anything more beautiful than Carol's deep faith in her Savior, who comforted her throughout her illness and journey Home," Margaret said tenderly.

"Honestly," I said as tears welled in my eyes. "I don't know whether to weep tears of sadness or tears of joy. Carol's death made all of us so sad, yet now, knowing what really happened to Carol makes my heart leap for joy."

Margaret and I sat quietly, thinking about Carol. It was now dark, and a full moon was beginning its trek through the night sky. Its bright, bluish hue seemed to increase the wondrous radiance of Margaret's glittering white gown.

After a while, Margaret said softly, "When Jesus was preparing his disciples for his upcoming death and resurrection, he told them that they would indeed experience sorrow. He said to them, 'Truly, truly I say to you, you will weep and lament, but the world will rejoice. You will be sorrowful, but your sorrow will turn into joy. I will see you again, and your hearts will rejoice, and no one will take your joy from you.' *Joy* was part of God's intended message for you, dear Jenn, when he permitted you to have this extraordinary dream. This is what he wanted you to know:

> *"Do not be afraid of death, dear child, for it is your way back home to me. I have commanded my angels to watch over you, and you will not make the crossing alone. I await your return with great joy."*

I shook my head in wonder. I had never considered that the separate concepts of death and joy could exist together as one poignant truth . . . until now.

When Worlds Collide

Look! I am creating new heavens and a new earth, and no
one will even think about the old ones anymore. Be glad;
rejoice forever in my creation!

ISAIAH 65:17–18

So we fix our eyes not on what is seen, but on what is
unseen, since what is seen is temporary, but what is unseen
is eternal.

2 CORINTHIANS 4:18

The full moon had reached its zenith in the night sky, transforming my backyard into a magical wonderland of shadow and light. It was a perfect setting for the wondrous revelations my angel had just provided about death and life. "This journey of ours has revealed so many things I never completely understood, Margaret," I said. "I am truly amazed to learn how many times the heavenly realm has intersected with my life."

Margaret flashed me her lovely smile. "Heaven *wants* to intersect with you, child. You were not created to go through the human experience alone—heaven wants to walk alongside you, providing wisdom, help, and hope." Then she gave me a knowing look. "You had a special visit with your friend after she returned to her heavenly home, didn't you?"

"I sure did," I answered. I leaned my head back and gazed up at the moon and began to tell her about an intriguing dream visit I'd had with Carol a month after she died.

I approach a charming, white, cottage-style house with a large, inviting front porch. The air is pleasant and warm. As I begin climbing the steps to the front door, the screen door opens and there stands my friend Carol, wearing a cheerful red-and-white apron. Her curly, near–shoulder-length white hair dances slightly in the breeze, and her cheeks are a rosy pink. She has a fresh-baked-cookie smell about her. She looks wonderful and happy. She gives me a big smile and comes out to greet me. "Jennifer!" she says, her eyes sparkling with excitement. "I am so glad you came to see me! I have so much to tell you. Heaven is not what I expected—it is so much more."

Carol tells me that heaven is not just a remote place away from earth. Heaven is everywhere—an unseen world that exists alongside ours. It surrounds us and moves with us each and every day of our existence on earth, yet we are separated by a barrier put in place by God. She tells me that Jesus can cross over to earth any time he is needed. His angels can do the same. Their bodies are able to cross the barrier between heaven and earth, whereas humans, by nature of our sinful flesh, cannot. When we are set free in death, we can then cross the barrier into our heavenly home. Even more glorious is the fact that there is a steady, continuous merging occurring between earth and the realm of heaven, as if the barrier is slowly thinning. God is establishing his kingdom in the hearts of believers—throughout the ages, one at a time.

I listen in amazement to all that Carol is telling me, and it resonates inside me as a mind-boggling truth. As I stand there on the porch, the images begin to fade and I awaken.

As I finished describing this dream, I marveled that heaven *was* intersecting my real world in powerful ways . . . realms colliding, Jesus appearing, angelic interventions . . .

Breaking my reverie, Margaret quietly asked, "What are your impressions of this dream visit you had with Carol?"

"Honestly," I replied, shaking my head slowly, "I feel truly blessed by what she shared with me. To begin with, since I knew Carol was now Home, in my mind's eye I saw her in the charming setting of a cottage-style home with a large veranda-like front porch, a type of home that is particularly appealing and comforting to me. And when she came out onto the porch to greet me, she was so happy and excited to share something that gave her great delight. As she shared her thoughts with me, I began to understand them with a clarity I had not experienced before.

"Carol told me that heaven is everywhere, all around us. It makes me immediately think of that moment you and I had here in the back of the yard when we embraced heaven together."

Margaret beamed, her eyes sparkling, and I continued.

"It makes sense to me, Margaret. I used to think of heaven as somewhere 'up there,' far, far away. In the very first chapter of Genesis it states that heaven and earth are separate, separated by a barrier put in place by God. And that is true. We cannot see heaven, and we cannot go there until we are set free from our earthly bodies. I still think of heaven as 'up' since anything not *on* earth is *above*. But I do not believe that heaven is far away. Especially after all I have learned from you."

Margaret gave me a delighted smile. "When you consider that heaven, though separate from earth, is everywhere, it can help you understand that *God is everywhere*. He sees your actions, and he knows what is in your hearts and minds. He is with you all the time. And when you choose to be in a relationship with him, he sends his Spirit across the barrier to live within you, to guide you, to be your advocate and comforter."

"The way you explain it sounds so simple, Margaret," I said thoughtfully, "and yet it seems heaven is such a difficult concept for people to grasp. Or maybe grasp isn't the right word—maybe it's just hard to believe. It is hard to believe in something you can't see."

"Ah, yes," said Margaret with a wistful smile. "You cannot believe in something *until you give yourself permission to believe.* That, child, is true freedom."

"I love that!" I exclaimed. "It gives me the freedom to believe that anything is possible when it comes to the things of God."

"Hold on to that belief, dear girl," laughed Margaret. "Let's get back to your visit with Carol. What else did she say that enlightened you?"

"Well," I answered, "Carol did not mention it specifically, but one of her revelations stirred a more profound awareness in me regarding the essential nature of *prayer*. She told me our Lord can cross over to earth anytime he is needed. It's as if God provided his children with a powerful lifeline to heaven . . . a way to communicate with him—through prayer—across the barrier between earth and heaven. When we cry out to him, he can respond in an instant."

With a nod of approval, Margaret's tone became serious. "Communication is crucial to the success of any relationship, Jennifer, both here on earth and in heaven. Our beloved Heavenly Prince was in constant prayer during his time on earth. He knew the value of and necessity of prayer, because it was his lifeline to his Father and his true home. My child, *even though God is all-seeing, he still wants to hear from you.* He wants to know about the desires, joys, and concerns of your heart, and he wants you to ask him for help, for blessings, for spiritual gifts. Because when you do so, you are *choosing* to have a relationship with him; you are choosing to grow closer to him and to put your trust in the one who has loved you since the very beginning. *That* is what brings our Father immeasurable joy."

"I can't imagine *not* talking to God," I said. "I talk to him all the time. I told you earlier how Billy Graham encouraged me to talk to God and how that changed my life. Throughout the years, as I have grown into my relationship with him, I have experienced spine-tingling examples of the Divine nature of prayer."

"Can you share one of those examples with me?" asked Margaret.

"Sure," I said. "This was an experience I will never forget. I was working for a hospital system in Ohio when the Alfred P. Murrah Federal Building in Oklahoma City was bombed. It was a homegrown terrorist attack, and it left the nation reeling. Our faith-based hospital had a sister hospital in Oklahoma City where many of the injured were being treated and many of the dead had been taken. In an effort to express our love and concern for our counterparts who were caring for the victims and their families, we posted a huge banner in our lobby to provide a way for our employees, patients, and visitors to share their thoughts and prayers. The long banner hung for a week, and every inch was filled with written prayers. It was beautiful and breathtaking. One short prayer particularly touched my heart: 'May God wrap your hospital, and all who are within its walls, in his loving embrace.'

"Finally, the banner was carefully taken down and rolled up, ready for its journey to Oklahoma City. I was asked by our administrator to take the banner over to the other hospital in our system where it would be shipped from. My job frequently took me to this other hospital, and I planned to go over later in the day. I carried the banner back to my office and set it in the corner up against the wall behind my desk.

"As I sat down and got back to work, I was continually distracted by the feeling of a presence in the room. It was so strong that several times I swung around in my chair and looked toward the wall. I could see nothing but the scroll of prayers standing silently there, where I had placed it. But each time I turned my back to it, the little hairs on the back of my neck stood on end. *Someone or something unseen was there in the room with me.* It was then that I realized that prayers truly have a life of their own. They are not just words written down on paper, or words casually spoken. Prayers are like living bursts of energy and are carried straight to the throne of heaven. And it's my guess that angels help carry our requests to the throne of the Most High. I don't know that for sure, but I do know that for the rest of the afternoon *I was in the presence of something holy.* And I have a feeling that God heard every single one of those loving petitions."

Margaret nodded and said reverently, "Prayers are precious offerings, Jennifer, and you can be assured that they are indeed carried by the heavenly host to the throne room of God. Listen to this moment in scripture from Revelation: 'Another angel, who had a golden censer, came and stood at the altar. He was given much incense to offer, with the prayers of all God's people, on the golden altar in front of the throne. The smoke of the incense, together with the prayers of God's people, went up before God from the angel's hand.' Not only does God hear the petitions of his beloved, he directs all under his authority to act on them."

Now my spine tingled again! "I believe that, Margaret. In my dream, Carol said the same thing—when we are in need and cry out to him, God hears and he acts. A close friend of mine told me a wonderful true story about three friends—Jenny, Margie, and Gina—that is a good example of this."

"Do tell," encouraged Margaret.

"Jenny suffered from a serious chronic lung disorder. One Friday night she was hospitalized and became comatose. Her daughter was advised that if things did not improve overnight, the family should be called in. More than eight hundred miles away that same Friday night and early Saturday morning, Margie had been deep in prayer for her friend Jenny. She intended to wait until a little later in the morning to call Jenny's daughter for an update on her condition. Meanwhile, early Saturday morning, Gina, another friend, decided to stop in to visit Jenny in the hospital. Gina was a believer, but was without a church home and at a point in her life where she longed for a deeper relationship with God; she needed to take her faith to another level.

"When Gina entered the hospital room, several miracles occurred at once. As she approached Jenny's bed, she was amazed to see an angel sitting at the head of the bed, stroking Jenny's hair! Gina knew instinctively that, no matter what happened, Jenny was going to be okay. At this same moment, many miles away, a worried Margie couldn't wait any longer and decided to call Jenny's daughter a little earlier than she'd planned for an update. When she placed her hand on the phone to make the call, Margie was overtaken with joy and a revelation that Jenny was going to recover. Laughing and with a relieved smile on her face, she placed the call to Jenny's daughter and told her that she already knew Jenny was going to be fine. And she was right! Jenny did indeed recover."

"That is a wonderful story, because you can see how our Heavenly Father ministered to each of these three women *in a single instant*! He answered Margie's prayer, and he sent his messenger to comfort Jenny *and* to enrich Gina's faith. And think about Gina—*God opened her eyes so that she could see.* Imagine the leap her faith took in that very moment. Oh, that is just the tip of the iceberg, my sweet child," Margaret exclaimed, the radiance around her growing suddenly brighter. "The Almighty is so powerful and so generous with his grace that he can respond all over the *world* in an instant."

I sighed and tipped my head back in my chair. What Margaret just said was pretty mind-boggling. I couldn't help but feel God's presence as I gazed up at the great expanse of moon and stars, knowing he created all of it. And as vast as the universe is, God cares enough to be available whenever we need him. Margaret's very presence sitting next to me here in my backyard was proof of that.

"A penny for your thoughts?" Margaret's question brought me back from my reverie.

"I am feeling overwhelmed by God's love and care for us, Margaret. When I visited with Carol in my dream, she had the same sense of excitement and anticipation about her that I have sensed in others I have had visits from. She knows that much more is going to happen in God's plan for us and for those in heaven. It is so exciting to know we are part of a plan that is still unfolding, a plan that holds many wonders for us. Remember that feeling of excited anticipation I felt in my dream about being on a journey? That is the kind of feeling I am experiencing now, but this time I am not dreaming."

Margaret laughed. "Believe it or not, Jenn, all of us in heaven are experiencing the same kind of excitement you describe."

I sighed, gazing up at the twinkling universe. "I wish I had a telescope that would enable me to see much further into God's creation—to see galaxies and far-off worlds. When I recall what Carol told me about God establishing his kingdom in the hearts of believers, I imagine watching two worlds slowly merging together, like pictures I have seen from the Hubble Space Telescope. *That* would be amazing to watch!"

"We *are* watching it happen, dear one," said Margaret with a mysterious smile.

I got goose bumps again.

Margaret continued. "Jenn, when Jesus made the statement 'the kingdom of heaven is at hand,' he was speaking a profound truth. *Jesus is that place where the two realms meet . . . the exact center of the intersection of heaven and earth.* God is, at this very moment, establishing the heirs of his Kingdom through Jesus and the Holy Spirit, who dwell in the hearts of all believers. And, as an heir to the King, *you, dear girl, are a princess of his royal household*! It is a great privilege that carries with it great responsibility."

A princess. That made my heart smile. "I think I know what that responsibility is, Margaret," I said. "As beloved children of the Father, we are to share with others the wonders of a life in Christ, so that they may be heirs to the Kingdom with us."

"Yes," affirmed Margaret. "And when his Kingdom comes, what a glorious event that will be. In the book of Revelation, the apostle John frequently refers to the new heaven and the new earth and describes his visions of them. 'Then I saw a new heaven and a new earth . . . And I saw the Holy City, new Jerusalem, coming down out of heaven from God . . . And I heard a loud voice from the throne saying, 'Behold, the dwelling place of

God is with man. He will dwell with them, and they will be his people, and God himself will be with them as their God.'

"On this day, heaven and earth will be renewed and finally merged together. God himself will dwell among us. We will all dwell *together*, Jenn."

That brought a big smile to my face. "I cannot even imagine how wonderful that day will be," I said. "You, and these dreams about Carol, have taught me so much. As I view my life with this future in mind, it changes my whole perspective of my journey here on earth—why I am here and where I am heading. *I believe the single most important action in my life is to develop an intimate, deeply personal relationship with my Father in heaven.* And the purpose of my life here on earth is to continue to deepen that relationship at every level of my being, in heart, mind, and spirit; to be a careful and considerate caretaker of God's creation; to use the spiritual gifts he has given me; to learn right living from the words of his holy scriptures; to teach others about him; to listen to my heart and nurture the things that bring me joy; to serve others and to become a person who reflects his image. Knowing that our future is eternal fills me with hope and a great sense of anticipation. What a magnificent journey we are all on, my angel friend!"

Ah, my girl," sighed Margaret wistfully, "I am proud of you! You are *getting it!*" Then she reached over and placed her hand gently on my arm. "How wonderful and how marvelous that God sent these revelations to you through a faithful sister in Christ. Why he chose Carol to speak to you is known only to him. You never know where his next message will come from, but in his mysterious way, it will come in a form that is special and perfect, just for you.

"Listen now, Jenn, to your King's whisper as he lovingly places his royal robe around your shoulders:

"Open your eyes and see that heaven embraces you, my beloved. I am all around you—so close that before you call, I will answer. The day is coming when we will live together in a glorious Kingdom—a new place, more wonderful than you could ever imagine. Trust in me, for my faithfulness endures forever."

As I listened, I felt a sudden tingling sensation all over my body. I peered down at my arms and noticed they were glowing just the slightest little bit. Then my clothes began to glow. Startled, I looked over at Margaret. The radiance I had noticed coming from her gown and her body was now spreading over to me!

Margaret laughed and said, "Don't worry, sweet girl, I thought I would share just a bit of heaven's glory with you. When I left you for a while today, I spent time with the Almighty in his throne room. The radiance you noticed about me comes from the reflection of the glory of God himself. Everything in heaven, Jennifer, radiates with the reflection of his glory—*everything*. And when God reunites all of us together in the new heaven and earth, there will be no need for sunlight, because we will be lit by his Almighty presence."

I smiled and hugged my arms to my chest, soaking in the

glory of God that she shared with me. I did not want this moment to end, ever.

But Margaret stood and prepared to leave me for the night.

"It has been a long day for you, dear child," she said. "It is hard to believe it was just a few hours ago that our angel friends gave you a brief glimpse of the heavenly gateway as they left here to return Home. We've covered a lot of ground since then. You must get some rest now."

Looking back on our day together, I could not believe how much had happened. It was uncanny how being with Margaret made time appear to slow down. Although completely exhilarated from experiencing God's glory, I realized that, indeed, I was getting very sleepy.

"Okay, Margaret." I yawned without squeaking. "Will you be here in the morning?"

"Oh, yes," she replied. "And I am looking forward to it already. I've become very fond of our poolside chats. Have the umbrella up for us. I have a feeling it is going to be another warm day. Good night, dear one. May your Heavenly Prince give you a good rest."

Margaret's words floated on the air behind her as she moved toward the St. Francis statue and disappeared, her soft, glowing radiance slowly fading into the dark, leaving only the scent of white roses behind.

The Language of God

Suddenly, there was a sound from heaven like the roaring of
a mighty windstorm, and it filled the house where they were
sitting. Then, what looked like flames or tongues of fire
appeared and settled on each of them. And everyone
present was filled with the Holy Spirit and began speaking
in other languages, as the Holy Spirit gave them this ability.

ACTS 2:2–4

Refreshed by a wonderful night's sleep, I awakened early,
poured myself a cup of coffee, and sat at the kitchen table, savoring the quiet of the morning. Gazing through the window, I
could see that it was another beautiful Texas dawn. The sky was
streaked with a pink blush and the grass glistened with dew. I
watched with amusement as three little bluebirds raced through
the yard, playing a game of chase with one another. Guy and I
have affectionately named these birds Larry, Curly, and Moe,
after the Three Stooges, because of their funny antics. We have
watched them leave the nest and learn the necessities of life
together—flying, feeding, and most recently, how to drink and
take a birdbath.

This morning Larry, Curly, and Moe flew over to the tall, elegant fountain in the back of the yard. Water gently gurgled from the top of the urn that the graceful statue has hoisted on her shoulder. All three birds perched on the edge of the urn and took turns hopping into the water, merrily splashing their feathers. I grabbed my binoculars and hurried out onto the back porch to get a better look. Now I could hear their sweet little chirps as they played in the water. A shimmer of pink entered my vision in the binoculars, and I lowered them from my face to see what had caught my attention. I could only smile and shake my head because, of course, there was Margaret standing by the fountain. She was truly a feast for the eyes this morning. Her gown was a perfect, cotton candy pink, capturing the pink blush of the sky, and it glittered and sparkled, creating the illusion of tiny little prisms that reflected the morning light. I wished she could bring me a bolt of that fine fabric from heaven!

Again using the binoculars, I watched as Margaret raised her arms shoulder height and cupped her hands. Without any hesitation whatsoever, Larry, Curly, and Moe all hopped off the fountain right into her hands and sat there, twittering gaily at her. I could hear Margaret's merry laugh as she held the darling little bluebirds. They were so content. It was as if they could sense their Creator in her presence. Then, with a gentle flick of her hands, she released them into the air, and they hopped back onto the fountain and resumed their splashy bathing ritual.

"Good morning, Jenn!" called Margaret cheerily as she began to walk toward me. I waved to her and put down the binoculars. Then, remembering her request before she left last night, I stepped over to the garden table and raised the umbrella.

"Ah, what a glorious day the Lord has made." Margaret sighed as she settled into a chair. Her small, bare feet and the bottom of her gown were damp with dew. She looked at me and gave a smile that showed all of her perfect white teeth. "I will join you in a cup of coffee, Jenn, while we still have the cool breeze of the morning upon us."

I grinned at the not-so-subtle hint and left the lovely vision in pink sitting under the umbrella while I went to fetch our coffee. As I opened the door to the house, Cody burst through, almost knocking me off my feet in his haste to get outside and say hello.

When I stepped back outside carrying two steaming mugs, Cody was happily licking Margaret's hands and toes, his tail wagging back and forth at lightning speed. "Sorry for the doggy kisses, Margaret!" I called. "That is just Cody's way of saying hello."

"Oh, it is a lovely way to say hello." Margaret giggled. "It tickles."

I laughed with her and said, "Cody has a unique talent for communicating special things to people. He is kind of like Scooby-Doo."

"Scooby-Doo?" Margaret asked. Then she held up a finger and said quickly, "Wait a minute!" then closed her eyes and sat very still for a few seconds. Then she laughed out loud and clapped her hands. "Ruh-ro! What a very funny dog Scooby-Doo is. So, Jenn, how is Cody like Scooby-Doo?"

"Well," I replied with a twinkle in my eye, "Cody can tell you that he loves you."

"Oh, how fun!" Margaret laughed and clapped her hands again. "Show me!"

I pulled a treat from my pocket and gave it to Margaret. I instructed, "Show Cody the treat and say to him, slowly and distinctly, 'I . . . love . . . you.'" Cody sat expectantly in front of Margaret, and when she did as I had instructed, Cody cocked his head and said roughly in three distinct syllables, "Rhy Rhuv Rhroo!"

"Ooooooh! Good boy!" Margaret squealed in delight and gave Cody his treat. "That is wonderful! It must be very difficult for a dog to learn to say human words, and he did it very well indeed."

Margaret and I settled happily back into our chairs and watched as Cody raced off in search of squirrels to chase. We sipped our coffee and sat in quiet fellowship for several minutes, relishing the soft, cool breeze we knew wouldn't last much longer.

Margaret spoke first, breaking our quiet reverie. "You know, Jenn, as I listened to the birds' sweet chirps as they sat in my hands, and then as I heard Cody tell me "I love you," I am reminded of how God speaks to, and through, all of his creation, in many different languages. Each language is uniquely special to the one with whom he is communicating. Earlier, you mentioned an experience you had with a language you did not understand. I think this would be a good time to talk about it, don't you?"

"I guess so," I agreed with a sigh. Timidly, I looked down at my feet, and I could feel my stomach churn in anticipation of talking about something largely misunderstood by many people.

Margaret set her coffee cup down on the table, then reached over and took the cup out of my hands and placed it on the table next to hers. I got the feeling she wanted my full attention. She did. With her hands she gently tipped my chin up so that I was looking into her beautiful, wise face. And in Margaret's blue eyes I found the courage I needed.

I spoke softly. "All those years ago, by the bedside in Michigan, at the moment I asked Jesus to come into my life, the first thing that happened to me was that I was filled with an overwhelming joy and began to speak in a language I did not recognize. My aunt and uncle explained that this was the gift of tongues, of speaking in the Spirit. It is an experience that's hard to describe, but every time I am moved to speak in the Spirit, it fills me to overflowing and pours out of me. Even though it is mysterious, I have always felt this was an important gift for me and I have guarded it carefully, keeping it very private."

Still holding me fast in her gaze, Margaret asked, "Why do you think this gift is important, child?"

"It was my first gift from God, and it felt so personal and special. Even though I did not know what I was saying, I felt that I was speaking in a language only God could understand. I know there are those who are gifted with the interpretation of tongues, but that was not given to me. But that doesn't seem to matter, because when I use this gift—when I am speaking this unknown language—I am filled with a peace that goes beyond my under-standing."

"Dear one, that is because this gift is an actual manifestation of the Holy Spirit that dwells within you. *The Spirit is real and active, speaking to you and for you. When you speak in the Spirit, you are communicating with the very heart of God.* Listen to this scripture from Corinthians: 'For one who speaks in a tongue does not speak to men but to God; for no one understands him, but he utters mysteries in the Spirit.'"

Margaret's words brought tears to my eyes.

"I have always deeply treasured this gift, Margaret," I said. "Even though I have come across people throughout my life who scoff at it. It has been hurtful to me to participate in conversa-tions when this subject comes up for discussion. I can feel my heart and spirit quicken as I think maybe, just maybe, I will be able to share my experience with it. But before I ever get the chance, someone will laugh at or criticize the gift of tongues, saying things like, 'It's all fake,' or 'I would never want that gift—it is too weird.' I find myself feeling humiliated and sad that I cannot speak without being ridiculed, so I say nothing at all. I am ashamed that I have not been a very good witness for my Lord."

"I am so sorry," Margaret said softly, her eyes reflecting the disappointment I felt. "Unfortunately, people criticize what they do not understand. And what they do not understand is the gift of tongues is a Divine form of communication that has been active for thousands of years. Jesus' disciples received this gift during Pentecost, when the Holy Spirit came to mankind just as he had promised. The ability to speak in the *language of God* enabled them and others to teach the good news about Jesus to people of foreign tongues all around the earth. And it has enabled you, Jenn, to speak to God with your heart when words fail you. Am I right?"

"That is true," I agreed. "There are times when I am deep in prayer for someone, and am at a loss for words. I may be praying for someone who is dying, and I wonder, what should I pray for? Should I ask God for healing? Should I pray for God to take them home and stop the suffering? In times like these, I feel moved to pray in the Spirit. And every time, as these mysterious words are flowing from deep within me and pouring out through my lips, I experience an *ancient presence, a wisdom beyond my own understanding* and *pure, unconditional love."*

Margaret smiled knowingly. "There is a scripture from Romans that speaks to this very point, Jennifer:

"Likewise the Spirit helps us in our weakness; for we do not know how to pray as we ought, but that very Spirit intercedes with sighs too deep for words. And God who searches the heart, knows what is in the mind of the Spirit, because the Spirit intercedes for the saints according to the will of God."

"That's lovely," I said wistfully. "It is comforting to know that the Spirit knows my heart and knows even better than I how to talk to my Heavenly Father. There have been many times in my life when I have gone to the Lord in prayer, when my heart was so heavy all I could do was sigh."

I heard a little sniffle and looked over at Margaret, who was wiping away a stray tear that had begun making its way down her cheek. I knew she understood completely the various heart-aches that had prompted those sighs.

After a few moments, Margaret spoke quietly. "In Romans, a word is used that points to an important characteristic of the Spirit living within you. That word is *intercede*. You recently ex-perienced an intercession of the Spirit when your father was going through a traumatic event. I am sure you remember this. It was a combination of two of your spiritual gifts—a dream and an alert to prayer by the Spirit."

"I certainly do remember, Margaret. It was another one of those extraordinary heavenly intersections. My father needed hip replacement surgery, and I traveled back to Ohio to be there for him and for my mother. The surgery went well, and Daddy was to stay in the hospital for about three days. While I was there, my sister asked me if I could stay at her house for a couple of days with their three children while she and her husband made a quick trip out of town to attend a charity event. Always happy to spend time with my nieces and nephew, I agreed, as long as my mother did not need me at home. Mother was spending most of her time at the hospital with Daddy, coming home only at night to eat and sleep, so she encouraged me to go spend time with the children.

"The first night at my sister's house, I settled into the comfy guest-room bed and fell fast asleep. It had been a long few days. While asleep, I had a dream."

I am at my parents' home and the phone begins to ring. As I start to pick it up I see that the phone number on the screen is from the hospital where Daddy is staying. I try to answer, but hear nothing. Thinking Mother has answered the call upstairs, I go up to ask if everything is okay. As I enter her room, she is scurrying around as if getting ready to go somewhere in a hurry. She tells me Daddy needs her right away, so she is going to go to him at the hospital. Next, I see Daddy in his hospital room, wildly thrashing around in his bed. Then Mother walks into his room and crawls up onto the bed with him. At that moment he becomes calm, and my dream ends.

"I awakened with a start and reasoned that I was just experiencing a delayed reaction to the normal anxiety anyone would feel after having a loved one go through surgery. But the dream disturbed me. I tried to go back to sleep but had no success, which was unusual for me. I looked at the clock, and it was three a.m. I had the feeling that something was not right and could not shake it. Finally, I began to pray, and after a while I just let the Holy Spirit pray through me in tongues, since I didn't really understand what was going on.

"At three thirty a.m., I finally felt released from whatever was keeping me up and in prayer. I promptly fell back to sleep and slept soundly until about eight a.m. I decided to call my mother at the house to check in with her before she left to go back to the hospital. She did not answer the house phone, so I tried her cell phone. She picked it up right away and spoke very softly, almost in a whisper. I asked where she was and she told me she was already at the hospital. Then she went on to say that she had received a call from my father in the middle of the night. He was having a bad reaction to the narcotics he had been given for pain and was very agitated. He pleaded with her to come and be with him, so she got dressed and drove to the hospital and was there with him by three thirty a.m. He was finally calm and sleeping soundly after a new medication had been administered.

"I remember thinking, *There you go again, God!* You would think I would be used to this by now, but episodes like this still fill me with awe. God permitted me to have another Divine dream and sent his Spirit to help me pray in the midst of this crisis my parents were experiencing."

Margaret's eyes sparkled with delight. "Awe is exactly what you should be feeling, Jenn, when the Holy Spirit intercedes according to the will of God. In this particular experience, God let you know in no uncertain terms that while this event was being played out, *he was all over it.* He was there in the room with your daddy, he was there at the house with your mother, and he was at your sister's house with you. The Almighty's love and care for his children is powerful and ever present. God is good!"

"All the time!" I responded with a happy heart. I picked up my coffee cup and sat back in my chair, savoring the taste and aroma of the fresh, strong brew. It was so freeing to be able to talk about this gift of the Spirit with someone so willing to listen.

Just then, in a breathtaking display of brilliant yellow and black, a large swallowtail butterfly left the flower he was feeding from nearby and perched delicately on the rim of Margaret's coffee cup. His wings gently moved up and down as he watched us. Margaret laughed softly and raised her face to the sky. I thought I saw her mouth a silent *Thank you!* so I peered around the umbrella and looked up to see whom she might be talking to. Of course, there was no one there.

"Margaret?" I began.

Margaret turned her eyes on me and said, "This, sweet girl, is a little gift for you from the Holy Spirit. Whenever you see this butterfly in your garden, he wants you to remember the transforming power of the Almighty and how his gifts can be used to transform the lives of his children.

"Just as the butterfly was transformed from a caterpillar into a beautiful creature, so *you* were transformed when you sought and accepted Jesus into your heart. And the gifts he gave you have empowered you to transform the lives of others. Your dreaming and the type of prayer in the Spirit you just described is a powerful form of intercession. Remember the dreams about your grandmother's fall and the baby with the heart condition? You have long wondered what you were supposed to do with that information. God has given you your answer, dear one. You are to intercede with prayer when prompted by your dreams and the Spirit."

I sat very still and realized that Margaret was absolutely right. I wished I could have realized that truth back when I had first experienced those dreams, so that I could have interceded in prayer for those I cared deeply about. I sighed with the acknowledgment that I really do sometimes take a long time to get it!

Margaret gave me a gentle smile, and I knew she understood. "Learning to use God's gifts is a process, Jenn. You have been faithful in your desire to learn from him, and he has been faithful to you in return. Jesus promised to provide the Holy Spirit, the comforter, advocate, and counselor, to his people once he had ascended into heaven. With this tremendous gift, he places a power in you that enables you to do more than you could ever imagine. Jesus said to his beloved disciples, 'Truly, truly, I say to you, whoever believes in me will also do the works that I do; and greater works than these will he do, because I am going to the Father.'

"The gifts of the Spirit, deeply rooted in love, are intimately designed for each believer in order that they may be used to bring about healing and restoration, encouragement in faith, and advancement of the Kingdom of God. So, dear child, let these words be written on your heart: *To whom much is given, much is expected.*"

The butterfly's wings continued their slow, rhythmic motion as I listened to Margaret's powerful words. What a beautiful creature it had become. Truly, transformation begets beauty, in a butterfly, and in the hearts of believers.

Margaret smiled as she watched me process her statement. Finally, with a little *"ahem!"* she gently guided my attention back to our conversation and continued. "I have provided you with only a glimpse of the beauty of one transformed by the Spirit of God. I pray that one day you will fully grasp the reality of how stunningly beautiful you are to the One who set his Spirit within you. I encourage you to cherish this truth. Now, listen, butterfly girl, as God speaks these words into the depths of your heart:

"When I promised that I would be with you to the end of the age, I meant it. To find me, look no further than inside yourself. Call upon me, my beloved, for in me, anything is possible!"

After letting me sit with these precious words for a few moments, Margaret asked, "Jenn, are you beginning to see how active the realm of heaven has been in your life? In your dreams, surrounding you, walking with you, guiding you, speaking to and for you . . . ?"

"Yes, I am, Margaret. You have shown me there have been so many of those heavenly intersections in my life. I feel like I have been walking around with blinders on, seeing part, but not all of the picture."

"To see clearly, child, you have to *want* to see clearly," said Margaret thoughtfully, "and I know that this has been a desire of your heart for a long time. There is something I want you to see now. Think back a minute. In the dream where you met Jesus, he held a candle for you and told you, 'I will always be here for you, Jennifer.' Then, in your dream about the beautiful child who was Jesus, as he waded into the lake he told you, 'I am going to my father now, but I will always be near if you need me.' In the same dream, when he was floating across from you in the flooding river, he said to you, 'Don't be afraid . . . You see? I am always here.' And in your dream about a pilgrimage, Jesus was your guide, walking right alongside you."

I gasped as a message emerged. It had been hiding away in my dreams until this very moment. This beautiful heavenly emissary sitting by my side had pulled these statements and events from my dreams throughout various stages of my life and helped me see them together as one profound truth. *I have nothing to fear, for heaven is with me always. And the Trinity—the Father, Son, and Spirit—will remind me of this as many times as I need to hear it!* My knees felt weak as I let that sink in. *Is it really possible to personally connect with and hear from my Creator? Yes! It most certainly is!*

Margaret gathered me in her arms and gave me a warm, delicious hug. "Congratulations, my girl. You have learned the lesson our Father has been teaching you all along. *Heaven truly is closer than you think.* The proof lives inside you in the many gifts of the Spirit he has provided."

Speechless, I clasped my hands to my heart and sat very still. Sensations of joy, tenderness, and awe swirled through me as I thought back over all that Margaret and I had talked about these past few days. The life experiences, the Divine dreams, God's quiet voice, the gifts of his Spirit, all interwoven by a common thread—his patient and consistent message of unconditional love for me and for all his children. *How could I have been so afraid to share my Divine encounters—God's active presence in my life—with others? This truth is so precious that the whole world needs to know about it.*

I could feel tears of gratitude forming as I realized I could not have taken this remarkable journey of discovery without God's help. What a wonderful gift Margaret had been to me.

My angel smiled as she noticed the big tears welling in my eyes.

"We all have much to be thankful for, Jennifer. We have a Father who loves us dearly. And I am so thankful he has given me the privilege of being your guardian angel and your guide. I have so enjoyed watching you grow, recognizing your gifts, and learning how to use them to bring glory to God. You will continue to learn, and I am looking forward to many more adventures together in the years to come."

The thought of more adventures with Margaret made me smile despite the tears.

Then Margaret's eyes suddenly lit up.

"I think this calls for a celebration. Oh yes! That is exactly what we need."

She clapped her hands together, bounded out of her chair, and practically skipped to the edge of the patio, where she stopped, hands on hips, and stared out over the yard.

I watched her, mystified. I could tell she was in big-time planning mode.

Margaret finally turned and faced me, her face glowing with excitement. "Remember the wonderful garden party you had for your birthday celebration?"

"Of course I do"—I laughed—"it was the party I had always dreamed of!"

"Well then, dear child, you are in for a double treat, because tonight we are going to have another party right here in your own backyard gardens." Margaret gleefully clapped her hands. "I am going to have to leave you for now because there is much to do to get ready. Look for me here after the sun goes down. *Oh, Jenn. We are going to have such a special evening!*"

I shook my head and laughed. It tickled me to see her so obviously excited. I managed to call out "Okay, I will see you tonight . . ." just before she shimmered and disappeared into thin air.

I stood up from my chair and looked out at the yard. A garden party hosted by an angel. That sounded, well . . . heavenly! Margaret's enthusiasm was contagious, because I began to feel the tickle-of-anticipation butterflies fluttering around in my tummy. I gathered up our empty coffee cups from the table and headed inside. Halfway to the house I stopped dead in my tracks and sucked in my breath.

"Oh my goodness gracious!" I exclaimed aloud. "What in the *world* am I going to *wear*?"

Garden Party

Awake, O north wind, and come, O south wind! Blow upon
my garden that its fragrance may be wafted abroad. Let my
beloved come to his garden and eat its choicest fruits.

SONG OF SOLOMON 4:16

The daylight hours seemed to stretch on forever as I attempted
to keep myself busy. Trying very hard not to count the minutes
until what promised to be an extraordinary evening, I caught up
on emails, took the dogs for a walk, and ran several errands. My
last stop was a visit to the craft store to purchase material to
make a blanket for a friend who was expecting a baby girl.
Spending time among the rows of soft, pastel-colored fleece
filled my mind with dreamy thoughts of "sugar and spice and everything nice," and before I knew it, the afternoon was over.

As the appointed hour of sunset approached, I walked to my
closet to pick out something to wear, I was still mystified . . .
what *does* one wear to a party hosted by an angel? Casual?
Dressy? As I snapped on the light, I gave a slight gasp. My decision had already been made for me. Hanging prominently on a
hanger before me was a beautiful pink dress that shimmered and

glistened in the light. It was a simple, elegant, three-quarter-length dress with long sleeves, a fitted bodice, and a slightly flared skirt. I realized the fabric was identical to the fabric of the gown Margaret had worn that morning . . . the gown I had so longingly admired! I quickly slipped on the dress. Of course, it fit perfectly.

The sun finally sank below the horizon and darkening shadows began their nightly trek across the lawn. I was so excited I could hardly bear it. I peered out the back door every minute or so, hoping to witness Margaret's return. Thirty minutes passed and still nothing. It was now dark. The night air was still quite warm, so I slipped into my bedroom one more time to pin my hair into a soft updo. Finally satisfied, I strolled back through my room, and my eyes caught a glimmer of something bright through the shutters on the windows. My breath caught in my throat as I hurried through the house and stepped out the back door onto the porch.

Words can hardly describe the vision that my eyes beheld. My backyard was completely transformed! All around the pool, on the patio, on the grass, and around the fire pit stood enormous white rosebushes. They glowed with an ethereal white light, and floating above and around each rosebush were several glowing white orbs, similar to votive candles. They slowly circled and danced among the roses, creating the most beautiful visual effect I have ever seen. The very air was tinged in a white luminescence and was saturated with the fragrance of the white roses mixed with sweet almond and night-blooming jasmine from my gardens. It was intoxicating!

As I stood there marveling, the space around my statue of St. Francis began to glow with the same ethereal white light. Margaret appeared first. Dressed in a lovely white gown, she sparkled like newly fallen snow in the moonlight. Around her waist she wore a loosely tied scarf that looked as if it were made from spun gold. I don't think I have ever seen her look more beautiful than she did tonight. As she stepped from the garden, two more angels appeared, dressed in the same sparkling white gowns, but these angels wore great, spun-gold sashes across their chests. They were tall and handsome, with dark-brown hair and radiant faces. My heart leapt for joy as I recognized them— they were the mighty warrior angels who were with Margaret and me just yesterday. As they approached, I noticed that one of the big angels carried a beautifully wrapped package in his mighty hands. A soft breeze began to rustle through the trees, prompting my wind chimes to sing their lovely lullaby, and the little tree frogs began their nightly chorus. The night sky was clear and the stars shined brightly overhead. *Oh my*—I breathed silently—*God sure knows how to set the stage for a lovely party!*

"Good evening, dear one," said Margaret, beaming, as she enveloped me in a big hug. "What a glorious night for a celebration. Our Heavenly Father sends you his dearest love and blessings, and he is so excited about tonight." My heart thrilled as I imagined my Lord's personal involvement in this evening. "I see you remember our friends, Jenn. They did not want to miss this special time with you. Come, let's all go sit down."

Margaret led us over to our table and chairs by the garden. As she walked with me, she leaned over and whispered mischievously in my ear, "I *love* your dress!" I gave her a playful nudge in response. Four chairs covered elegantly in white silk and ribbons were placed around the table. We sat down, surrounded by the white roses and dancing, glowing orbs. Margaret beamed as she caught me eyeing the beautifully wrapped gift as it was placed on the table.

"Yes, my dear child, this gift is for you, but if you can stand the suspense for just a little while longer, I have a special message for you from our Father."

I nodded, my excitement mounting.

Margaret stretched out her arms and opened her hands. "Let's all join hands together," she instructed quietly. I reached out my arms and placed each of my hands in the massive hand of one of the warrior angels—one on my left and one on my right—and then these angels joined their hands with Margaret. As we sat in silence for a moment, the most wondrous thing happened. All three angels began to glow with a radiant white light, and then it spread over to me, so that we all sat there at the little table, enveloped in the glory light of heaven.

Then Margaret began to speak in a gentle, clear voice. "I am honored, Jennifer, to have been your guide through this journey of your life's experiences and encounters with God. You have put away your fears and have come face-to-face with the reality that you are intimately connected to the Divine—you have never been apart from it. The realm of heaven came with you into this world and walks alongside you each and every day . . . teaching, guiding, and revealing the truths God needs you to know in order to live the abundant life he desires for you.

"On our journey together, you have opened yourself and made yourself vulnerable in order to discover how God has been present in your life. You have gained in the understanding of your spiritual gifts and now know how to use them to do your part in the advancement of the Kingdom. You have the power to help others discover that they, too, are God's beloved, and are never alone.

"What God desires more than anything else is for his children to seek him, to develop an intimate and prayerful relationship with him, to *ask* him for what they need in order to live full, joyful, complete lives. Oh, my dear child, our Father has so *much* to give to each of his children! You are the delight of his heart, and his dearest wish is to be the delight of *your* heart! This has been his plan since the very beginning."

My heart overflowed with love and humility as I sat there listening to Margaret's words. Fighting back the tears that were once again welling in my eyes, my gaze fell upon the wrapped package on the table, and I recalled a meaningful story about the gifts God wished to share with us.

"Margaret," I said, a little shyly, "something you said just now, about how God has so much he wants to give us, reminds me of a remarkable vision someone once shared with me. Would you like to hear about it?"

"We would love to," all three angels exclaimed at once. That made me smile. And so I told them about the *vision of the gifts*.

A woman sees herself in a room in heaven, and the room is filled with beautifully wrapped packages. As she wan-

ders around the room to get a closer look, she realizes that they all have her name on them. The Lord is standing there watching her, and she asks him, "Lord, what are these? Are they all for me?" The Lord replies, "Yes, child, they have been up here your entire life, just waiting for you to ask for them. When you ask for a gift, it is sent to you. These are the leftover gifts you have never asked for.

"This woman realized that she needed to free herself to ask God for his blessings and for the desires of her heart, because he so much wanted to give them. In fact, he has them all ready to send."

"That is an important lesson," said Margaret. "Remember when I told you at the beginning of our journey that I wanted you to approach it with the faith of a child?"

I nodded.

"When you were a child, I watched you receive your birthday and Christmas gifts with pure delight and expectation. And the gifts you received brought you joy, enrichment, and knowledge. That is how God wants his children to be, Jenn, with the gifts he is so willing to provide to you. He wants you to *ask* for whatever is in your heart with childlike expectation, and then joyfully open your arms to receive."

I thought about what Margaret said for a moment. "I think I have always had a hard time asking God for my heart's desires because I felt that they wouldn't be important enough to God. After all, he is *God* and has a lot more to worry about than me. But I love what you just said, because it reminds me that I am his child—the delight of his heart—of *course* he wants me to come to him with my needs and desires!"

My three angel friends smiled in approval. Then Margaret continued. "I have a suggestion for you, Jenn. Make a list of the deepest desires of your heart, pray over them with expectation, and then tuck them inside your Bible in Matthew chapter twenty-one, verse twenty-two, where it reads, 'Whatever you ask in prayer, you will receive, if you have faith.' Then, every few months or so, pull out your list and see how God has acted upon it. I think you will be astonished at the results. Just remember," she said, with a twinkle in her eye, "that God sometimes answers with something different from what you have asked for, because he knows you better than you know yourself."

The two warrior angels were nodding their heads enthusiastically as Margaret finished speaking. That made me smile!

"Let's get back to the party," Margaret said with a grin. "I have asked someone else to join our little celebration." She turned in her chair, looked out into the yard, and called, "Come on out, sweet babies!"

Suddenly I spied three little heads peeking out from behind one of the tall rosebushes. In response to Margaret's call, out pranced my three sweet dogs, wagging their tails. Each wore a beautiful white satin bow tied to its collar.

I clapped my hands. "Hannah! Isabel! Cody! You look fabulous!" My darling canine trio trotted over to our table and stood by each of the three angels.

"We could not have had the party without them, Jenn. They have so graciously shared their home and yard with us these past few days." Margaret directed her attention to the pups as they watched her with great interest. "And to show our thanks to you, little four-legged children, we have something for you."

A crystal bowl had appeared on the table and it was filled to the brim with heart-shaped dog treats. Each angel took a treat from the bowl and placed it on the table before them. Cody, using all the restraint he could muster, sat down before Margaret in his best 'sit,' and without any prompting pronounced three carefully formed syllables: "Rhy! Rhuv! Rhoo!"

Our two mighty angel friends roared with laughter. They asked simultaneously, "Do the other dogs talk, too?"

"No"—I laughed—"but they do a very nice doggy-speak when asked."

And sure enough, as each angel commanded them to speak, Hannah and Isabel responded brilliantly with a sharp *ruff*!

The laughter and *ruff*s lasted for a few more minutes until I noticed the bowl was practically empty of treats.

"I hate to be a party pooper," I scolded, "but these kiddos still have to eat their dinner. I think we have had enough treats for tonight."

Margaret sneaked one final treat to Cody and then stood up. "We can't let them leave without a blessing," she said, looking at them fondly. The other two angels stood and joined Margaret. Each angel placed a gentle hand on a dog's forehead. I was amazed at how quiet and still the dogs had become. Maybe they sensed the presence of their Creator in their new friends.

Margaret prayed, "May God bless and keep you, dear little ones, for all the days of your lives. May you always have sunshine to play in, treats to fill your tummies, and your momma's love to keep you warm and cozy at night. God loves you very much, Hannah, Isabel, and Cody."

After a few last pats and hand licks and tail wags all around, the pups trotted off to the porch, where they snuggled into their outside beds to wait for me. I was so touched that Margaret had included my sweet dogs in this special evening. She really knew my heart.

Next, Margaret picked up the gift from the table and came to stand by my chair. "Okay, Jennifer, now it is your turn for a treat." She looked fondly over at her heavenly companions and continued. "We spent quite a bit of time in the throne room with our Father today, discussing which gift would be the perfect one to give to you this evening. After all, as we just acknowledged, God has so *many* gifts to give to his children."

I nodded. The suspense was killing me.

Margaret then leaned down and placed the gift in my hands. It was wrapped in lovely pearl-white paper and tied with a light-blue satin ribbon. "We present this to you, Jennifer, with much love from the very heart of heaven. Go ahead, child, . . . open it!"

Their eyes shining like the stars, the angels watched as I carefully removed the ribbon and unwrapped the package. I lifted the cover from the box and looked inside . . . and *gasped*. A bright luminescence flooded out of the box, illuminating my face. As I peered closer for a better look at the contents, I realized that the box was full of tiny, shimmering, diamond-like crystals just slightly larger than grains of sand. It was breathtakingly beautiful . . . *but what was it?*

I looked up with a questioning gaze to see all three angels smiling at me, laughing softly with joy. Then Margaret spoke, answering my question before it could form on my lips. "This, Jennifer, is a very special gift. The box you hold in your hands contains *the seeds of hope.*"

My mouth dropped open in surprise. *I didn't know there really was such a thing!*

Margaret continued. "When we began this journey together, you expressed the desire to explore the mysterious Divine encounters you have experienced, and to understand the *reason* God was revealing his presence to you so profoundly. The answer to your question is sitting in this box in your hands, dear one. *God has been revealing himself to you so that you can reveal him to others. By sharing your Divine dreams and the encounters you have had with your Creator, you will be sowing these seeds of hope into the hearts and lives of countless others.* And each of these tiny seeds is inscribed with the promise you now know well . . . *I am with you always.*"

Tears really did begin to flow now. I was humbled, and honored, that God would entrust me with such a special endeavor.

With a tender smile, Margaret continued. "Hope must not be contained, so together, in a few moments, we are going to scatter these seeds. Your garden, Jennifer, will become a sacred garden, where the seeds of hope will rest and find nourishment. And as your testimony finds open and believing hearts, the seeds of hope will take root and grow. As they grow, their roots will spread deep and wide to search out new fertile ground. *This* is how hope spreads."

I had no words. Just more goose bumps.

"Come now . . . let's do this!" Margaret said excitedly, motioning for the rest of us to join her as she stepped through the rosebushes and walked into the yard. "Bring the box with you, Jenn," she called.

As we stood together in the deep backyard, I carefully tilted the box and poured the tiny, glowing seeds into the waiting cupped hands of each angel, and then poured some into my own. "Margaret," I whispered, "tell us when!" I could hardly breathe . . . this moment felt so *holy*.

As if reading my thoughts, Margaret lifted her cupped hands to the sky and pronounced in a clear voice "Let these words from Isaiah be fulfilled: 'For as the earth brings forth its sprouts, and as a garden causes what is sown in it to sprout up, so the Lord God will cause righteousness and praise to sprout up before all the nations.'"

Then she lowered her arms and with a bright smile said, "*Now!*"

With that, the four of us swung our arms in great arcs, releasing the tiny glowing seeds of hope. I watched as the seeds scattered all over my yard and gardens, shimmering and sparkling as they settled into the ground. For a sacred moment the ground looked like a mirror image of the twinkling heavens above us. Soon the shimmering stopped. The seeds were now at rest. *Waiting.*

We walked back to our table in silence, and after we were all seated, Margaret said softly, "It was no coincidence, Jenn, that God chose the setting of your garden for our journey together. His love for gardens is represented in Scripture from beginning to end. God created the Garden of Eden for his beloved children, Adam and Eve. He walked with them and talked with them in that beautiful place. This was the setting of perfect relationship between God and humanity until the Fall from Grace. The Garden of Gethsemane was a retreat of serenity and prayer for our beloved Jesus as he faithfully carried out the Divine will of the Father. The Garden Tomb, where Jesus was buried, became the most sacred place on earth when he emerged from the tomb alive, victorious over sin and death. Here in this garden, Grace was restored. And when the great I AM finally comes to dwell among his children once again in the new heaven and earth, a glorious new garden will spring forth from in front of his throne, a crystal clear river of the water of life lined on either side by the trees of life, laden with luscious fruits. This garden will celebrate the fully restored relationship between God and his beloved children.

"God rejoices in the time that he spends with you here in your garden, dear one. The roots of his love for you grow deeper than you could ever imagine. And it pleases him so much that your garden has been added to those nurturing these precious seeds of hope—hope that will lead his beloved children back into a relationship with him."

As she finished speaking, a gentle breeze began rustling the treetops, picking up in intensity as it brushed through the yard, ringing my wind chimes and rustling the leaves and blossoms of the white rosebushes with the sound of a melancholy sigh. I sensed a change in the air.

Before I could even say a proper thank-you for this wonderful evening, Margaret and the two mighty angels rose from the table. As she looked at me fondly, I knew she understood the feelings in my heart. I loved her so much and had treasured the moments we had here at this table, sharing coffee, laughter, tears, and stories of God's revealed truths. With a sinking feeling, I suspected that my beloved angel and her two friends were soon going to leave my backyard for the final time. I rose from my chair to join them.

Confirming my last thought, Margaret gently placed her hands in mine and looked into my eyes. "It is now time for us to return Home, for our assignment here is finished. You will see us again, for we are always with you—remember that I *am* your guardian angel! And who knows"—she winked mysteriously— "our Father may have other assignments for you and me in the future." Her blue eyes danced merrily as she smiled her beautiful smile and wrapped me in a big hug. Then she whispered, "Give your sweet Guy a hug from me, and tell him he will catch many fish with that believing heart of his."

I laughed in surprise as she released me. *Heaven had been listening to our conversation that night on the porch.*

I addressed the three dear angels standing in front of me. "Thank you, all of you," I said with a full heart. "This was a wonderful party, and your gift is precious to me. I will think of each of you every day as I sit out here in my garden. I love you all so much."

"We love you, too, Jennifer," all three said at once. That made me smile again. Each of the mighty warrior angels gave me a big, sweet, gentle hug, and then all three angels turned and retreated slowly back through the white rosebushes toward the statue of St. Francis.

As they shimmered and vanished in a soft glow of white light, my backyard was returned to its original setting—the roses and glowing, dancing lights were gone.

Feeling the return of those pesky tears, I breathed a deep sigh and walked over to where the angels had just departed. Something on the ground at the feet of St. Francis caught my attention. I smiled through my tears as I recognized what it was. There lay a beautiful white rose, with no thorns. Suddenly, the air around me was filled with a sweet, clear voice that could only belong to an angel, and to my delight, she was singing a hymn I dearly loved called "In the Garden" . . .

> *"I come to the garden alone, while the dew is still on the*
> *roses; and the voice I hear, falling on my ear; The Son*
> *of God discloses.*
> *"And he walks with me, and he talks with me, and he*
> *tells me I am his own, and the joy we share as we*
> *tarry there, none other has ever known . . . "*

I closed my eyes and let my mind fill with the image of Jesus smiling at me and holding my hand as we listened to the hymn together here in my own garden.

All too soon, Margaret's sweet, beautiful voice faded away, and I knelt down to pick up the white rose. As I stood and brushed the tears from my face, a smile formed on my lips as I looked at the rose in my hand. I knew just what to do with it.

Epilogue

It will be good for those servants whose master finds them
ready, even if he comes in the middle of the night or toward
daybreak . . . You also must be ready, because the Son of
Man will come at an hour when you do not expect him.

LUKE 12:38, 40 (NIV)

*Dappled sunlight sparkles through the tall pines of the dense
forest, and my footsteps make barely a sound on the soft carpet of
mossy earth. This looks a lot like the beloved Michigan pine forest
where I vacationed in my youth. I lift my head and breathe in the
pungent aroma of evergreen mixed with the musty smell of de-
caying leaves and pine needles. As I continue down the path I
come upon a large log-cabin lodge. It has two massive, hinged
wooden doors, standing wide open. I step through the great doors
and look around the interior of the lodge. Above me, a high-
beamed ceiling soars upward and meets at the center like an A.
The floor is made of strong wooden planks. There is no furniture
except for one thing that stands in the middle of the room directly
in front of me. It is a huge, long, rectangular wooden table. It is so
tall I can barely see over it.*

I sense movement and see a doorway on the wall to the left of the table, like a big pantry door. Someone is rummaging around inside. Then he steps out. It is Jesus! He moves along the table, busily arranging items and then returns to the pantry for more. Whatever he is doing, he is totally engrossed in it. Finally, he notices my presence, looks at me with a mixture of surprise and joy, and steps around the table to stand in front of me.

"Jennifer!" He exclaims, "You are early. As you see, I am still preparing things." He puts his arm around my shoulders and gently guides me outside. He turns me toward the forest, and I see hundreds of little log houses blending in so well with the trees that I did not notice them before. He motions to one of the houses and lovingly whispers in my ear, "Go home, child, and get yourself ready. When everything is prepared, I will call all of you to come and join me."

I head off toward the little house he has selected for me, full of anticipation for the feast he has so diligently been preparing.

· · · · ·

Will *you* hear him when he calls?

Acknowledgments

"A dream is a wish your heart makes . . ." Oh, Disney's Cinderella, you were so right! Several years ago, my heart had a dream . . . a dream to write a book I believed could offer the healing of God's love to the world. As I mentioned this dream to others, I was met by a perplexing reaction: "That's nice, honey . . . but just keep in mind that what you are doing is really writing this book for yourself and your own inner healing." In other words, don't set your hopes too high.

I really didn't know how to react. Sure, writing is therapeutic, but I had a dream and wasn't willing to settle for just a personal journal–writing experience. I believed in the message of my story and I believed in myself. So, I continued to follow my heart, wrote my manuscript, and looked for a way to get it out into the world. What a wake-up call that was!

As I tried to navigate the publishing market on my own, I soon became very discouraged. How was an inexperienced and unknown homemaker turned author going to make a dent in the impossible world of publishing?

Fortunately, I belong to a wonderful, Spirit-filled eleven-thousand-member church and turned my focus to promoting my story within the women's ministries. I was invited to lead discussions and speak to large groups, and I was well received. The sharing and healing I witnessed in each and every one of these venues confirmed that the dream of my heart was real and worthwhile. I just wished those experiences could be replicated on a much larger scale.

Then one day I was asked to speak to—of all things—a men's Bible study group . . . at six thirty in the morning at a popular breakfast spot. Not usually an early riser, I dragged myself out of bed and got there just in time to order a much-needed cup of coffee before the meeting started. Amazingly, my coffee sat mostly untouched because these men were fully engaged in my presentation, and before I knew it my time was up. As the men were leaving, one man stayed behind. He had listened intently, but was quiet and reserved, and showed little reaction during my presentation. Enter my veritable white knight!

This gentleman introduced himself as Frank Eakin of Eakin Films & Publishing, and I learned he also was a member of our church. Frank is the brilliance behind the *12 Years A Slave* best-selling book and audiobook, featuring Louis Gossett, Jr., which was the inspiration for the winner of the 2014 Oscar for Best Picture. He told me he had come to this meeting specifically to hear me speak about my story because he felt there was a dearth of engaging content in the faith market and had heard that I offered a fresh angle. He had held back his participation in our discussion because, while intrigued by my story, he was mostly focused on measuring my authenticity—his acid test to determine whether to lend his guidance. Apparently I passed the test, because he read my manuscript and offered to take my dream forward. I could not believe my ears, or this tremendous blessing that God had just placed in my lap.

From that moment on, Frank, a recognized marketing genius in digital publishing, became my trusted advisor, mentor, and friend. He opened his amazing network to me and has guided my vision into an exciting reality. His world-class team developed one of the most beautiful and engaging author websites in the publishing market . . . and then he made the impossible happen. Lightning in a bottle! This wide-eyed homemaker from Texas flew to New York City to sit in the recording session of my first audiobook . . . to listen to the words I had authored on my laptop months earlier narrated by *Today* show host and household name Kathie Lee Gifford! While in New York, Kathie Lee introduced us to the When God Winks series author SQuire Rushnell and his wife, actress and comedienne Louise DuArt, who, in turn, introduced us to the woman who would become my literary agent, Jennifer Gates.

Within a month's time, Ms. Gates informed us that major publishers were interested in publishing *Come to the Garden.* A whirlwind trip to New York City and Nashville ensued, resulting in a contract with Howard Books—an imprint of Simon & Schuster! Publisher Jonathan Merkh and editor Beth Adams were the perfect fit. Next, Frank assembled a fabulous coast-to-coast dream team to help promote and launch *Come to the Garden*—people with hearts and minds for the Kingdom, including Jessica Amato, Nicole Op Den Bosch, Coleen Barr, and Esther Bochner at Audible/Amazon—the merchandising and public relations team that took Frank's *12 Years a Slave* audiobook to number one. This dream team also includes Debra Deyan of Deyan Audio, the number one audiobook producer in the world; Lesley Burbridge of Rogers & Cowan, the premier entertainment firm in Hollywood; and Oscar-winner Louis Gossett, Jr. In Nashville, Ash Greyson of Ribbow Media Group, which manages social media for major studio films; Tracy Cole of Rogers & Cowan; and Jennifer Smith, PR for Howard Books. In Alexandria, LA, Charlotte Lyles, team support. In Austin, cover art photographer Sanjay N. Patel; graphic artist Justine Boyer of Barking Pixel; and videographers Nelson Flores and Clint Howell of ProductionFor. In Houston, Lifetime Movie Channel director Michelle Mower; screenwriter Casey Kelly; web designer Jasen Peterson; graphic designer Patricia Zapata; tour producers Wayne Wagner of Wagner Media and Jack Hattingh of Pointcloud Media; music composer Brad Sayles; audio engineer Todd Hulslander; and Gary Walston, team support.

Goodness. And this is just the beginning. . . . My dream, the wish that my heart made, could never have come this far without Frank Eakin, nor the countless family members, friends, and members of my church family at The Woodlands United Methodist Church, who have been my angels of encouragement. The faithful enthusiasm, prayers, and support—financial and advisory—have been an incredible blessing to me and to this project.

My story is a Cinderella story, and a Cinderella story would not be complete without a true love. My dear husband, Guy, has walked with me throughout this entire project and has been my faithful supporter, sounding board, critic, and encourager. What an amazing adventure we have been on together! And throughout this adventure, this li'l Texas homemaker turned author has learned a valuable lesson: *Don't give up on your dreams. When you believe in yourself, someone will believe in you.*

Scriptures and Other References

BOOK EPIGRAPH

"Stand firm then, with the belt of truth buckled around your waist, with the breastplate of righteousness in place, and with your feet fitted with the readiness that comes from the gospel of peace. In addition to all this, take up the shield of faith, with which you can extinguish all the flaming arrows of the evil one. Take the helmet of salvation and the sword of the Spirit, which is the word of God."

EPHESIANS 6:14–17 (NIV)

TILLING THE SOIL

"I pray that the eyes of your heart may be enlightened in order that you may know the hope to which he has called you, the riches of his glorious inheritance in his holy people."

THE APOSTLE PAUL, EPHESIANS 1:18 (NIV)

MARGARET

Are not all angels spirits in the divine service, sent to serve for the sake of those who are to inherit salvation?

HEBREWS 1:14 (NRSV)

THE ASSIGNMENT

All Scripture is inspired by God and is useful for teaching, for reproof, for correction, and for training in righteousness, so that everyone who belongs to God may be proficient, equipped for every good work.

2 TIMOTHY 3:16–17 (NRSV)

"Behold, the days are coming," declares the Lord God, "when I will send a famine on the land—not a famine of bread, nor a thirst for water, but of hearing the words of the Lord."

AMOS 8:11 ESV

FEARFULLY AND WONDERFULLY MADE

I have called you by name, you are mine.

ISAIAH 43:1 (ESV)

For you created my inmost being; you knit me together in my mother's womb. I praise you because I am fearfully and wonderfully made; your works are wonderful, I know that full well. My frame was not hidden from you when I was made in the secret place. When I was woven together in the depths of the earth, your eyes saw my unformed body. All the days ordained for me were written in your book before one of them came to be.

PSALM 139:13–16 (NIV)

THIRST

As a deer longs for flowing streams, so my soul longs for you, O God. My soul thirsts for God, for the living God.

PSALM 42:1–2 (NRSV)

Special Mention: Citizens of heaven statement is from Alcorn, Randy. *Heaven, Chapter 20*, 2004, Eternal Perspective Ministries. The statement is attributed to St. Augustine.

Why, even the hairs of your head are all numbered.

LUKE 12:7 (ESV)

Before I formed you in the womb I knew you, and before you were born I consecrated you; I appointed you a prophet to the nations.

JEREMIAH 1:5 (ESV)

HEART'S DELIGHT

Be still and know that I am God

PSALM 46:10 (ESV)

At once the angel was joined by a huge angelic choir singing God's praises:

Glory to God in the heavenly heights, Peace to all men and women on earth who please him.

LUKE 2:13-14 (MSG)

They held harps given them by God and sang the song of God's servant Moses and of the Lamb.

REVELATION 15:2-3 (NIV)

And then I heard every creature in heaven and on earth and under the earth and in the sea. They sang: "Blessing and honor and glory and power belong to the one sitting on the throne and to the Lamb forever and ever."

REVELATION 5:13 (NLT)

Shout for joy to the Lord, all the earth, burst into jubilant song with music; make music to the Lord with the harp, with the harp and the sound of singing!

PSALM 98:4-5 (NIV)

The Lord your God is in your midst, a mighty one who will save; he will rejoice over you with gladness; he will quiet you by his love; he will exult over you with loud singing.

ZEPHANIAH 3:17 (ESV)

LORD, HEAR MY PRAYER

Rejoice in the Lord always; again I will say, Rejoice. Let your gentleness be known to everyone. The Lord is near. Do not worry about anything, but in everything by prayer and supplication with thanksgiving let your requests be made known to God. And the peace of God, which surpasses all understanding, will guard your hearts and your minds in Christ Jesus.

PHILIPPIANS 4:4–7 (NRSV)

God, come close. Come quickly! Open your ears—it's my voice you're hearing! Treat my prayer as sweet incense rising; my raised hands are my evening prayers.

PSALM 141:1-2 (MSG)

ASK, SEEK, KNOCK

And I tell you, ask and it will be given to you; seek, and you will find; knock, and it will be opened to you. For everyone who asks receives, and the one who seeks finds, and to the one who knocks it will be opened.

LUKE 11:9–10 (ESV)

But those who drink the water I give will never be thirsty again. It becomes a fresh, bubbling spring within them, giving them eternal life.

JOHN 4:14 (NLT)

Just so, I tell you, there is joy before the angels of God over one sinner who repents.

LUKE 15:10 (ESV)

You shall love the Lord your God with all your heart and with all your soul and with all your might.

DEUTERONOMY 6:5 (ESV)

Dream Girl

I slept, but my heart was awake.

SONG OF SOLOMON 5:2 (ESV)

There is a God in heaven who reveals mysteries and he has made known to King Nebuchadnezzar what will be in the latter days. Your dream and the visions of your head as you lay in bed are these. . . .

DANIEL 2:28 (ESV)

Call to me and I will answer you, and will tell you great and hidden things that you have not known.

JEREMIAH 33:3 (ESV)

Ears to hear and eyes to see—both are gifts from the Lord.

PROVERBS 20:12 (NLT)

EYE OF THE STORM

And he said, "Go out and stand on the mount before the Lord." And behold, the Lord passed by, and a great and strong wind tore the mountains and broke in pieces the rocks before the Lord, but the Lord was not in the wind. And after the wind an earthquake, but the Lord was not in the earthquake. And after the earthquake a fire, but the Lord was not in the fire. And after the fire the sound of a low whisper. And when Elijah heard it, he wrapped his face in his cloak and went out and stood at the entrance of the cave.

1 KINGS 19:11–13 (ESV)

SAVIOR

In the beginning the Word already existed. The Word was with God, and the Word was God. He existed in the beginning with God. God created everything through him, and nothing was created except through him. The Word gave life to everything that was created, and his life brought light to everyone. The light shines in the darkness, and the darkness can never extinguish it.

JOHN 1:1–5 (NLT)

Then Moses called all the elders of Israel and said to them, "Go and select lambs for yourselves according to your clans, and kill the Passover lamb. Take a bunch of hyssop and dip it in the blood that is in the basin, and touch the lintel and the two door-posts with the blood that is in the basin. None of you shall go out of the door of his house until the morning. For the Lord will pass through to strike the Egyptians, and when he sees the blood on the lintel and on the two doorposts, the Lord will pass over the door and will not allow the destroyer to enter your houses to strike you. You shall observe this rite as a statute for you and for your sons forever. And when you come to the land that the Lord will give you, as he has promised, you shall keep this service. And when your children say to you, 'What do you mean by this service?' you shall say, 'It is the sacrifice of the Lord's Passover, for he passed over the houses of the people of Israel in Egypt, when he struck the Egyptians but spared our houses.'" And the people bowed their heads and worshiped. Then the people of Israel went and did so; as the Lord had commanded Moses and Aaron, so they did. At midnight the Lord struck down all the firstborn in the land of Egypt, from the firstborn of Pharaoh who sat on his throne to the firstborn of the captive who was in the dungeon, and all the firstborn of the livestock. And Pharaoh rose up in the night, he and all his servants and all the Egyptians. And there was a great cry in Egypt, for there was not a house where someone was not dead. Then he summoned Moses and Aaron by night and said, "Up, go out from among my people, both you and the people of Israel; and go, serve the Lord, as you have said. Take your flocks and your herds, as you have said, and be gone, and bless me also!" The Egyptians were urgent with the people to send them out of the land in haste. For they said, "We shall all be dead." So the people took their dough before it was leavened, their kneading bowls being bound up in their cloaks on their shoulders. The people of Israel had also done as Moses told them, for they had asked the Egyptians for silver and gold jewelry and for clothing. And the Lord had given the people favor in the sight of the Egyptians, so that they let them have what they asked. Thus they plundered the Egyptians.

EXODUS 12:21-36 (ESV)

WHISPERED BLESSINGS

And the Lord called Samuel again the third time. And he arose and went to Eli and said, "Here I am, for you called me." Then Eli perceived that the Lord was calling the young man. Therefore Eli said to Samuel, "Go, lie down, and if he calls you, you shall say, 'Speak, Lord, for your servant hears.'" So Samuel went and lay down in his place. And the Lord came and stood, calling as at other times, "Samuel! Samuel!" And Samuel said, "Speak, for your servant hears."

1 SAMUEL 3:8–10 (ESV)

And there was a woman who had had a discharge of blood for twelve years, and who had suffered much under many physicians, and had spent all that she had, and was no better but rather grew worse. She had heard the reports about Jesus and came up behind him in the crowd and touched his garment. For she said, "If I touch even his garments, I will be made well." And immediately the flow of blood dried up, and she felt in her body that she was healed of her disease. And Jesus, perceiving in himself that power had gone out from him, immediately turned about in the crowd and said, "Who touched my garments?" And his disciples said to him, "You see the crowd pressing around you, and yet you say, 'Who touched me?'" And he looked around to see who had done it. But the woman, knowing what had happened to her, came in fear and trembling and fell down before him and told him the whole truth. And he said to her, "Daughter, your faith has made you well; go in peace, and be healed of your disease."

MARK 5:25–34 (ESV)

Have this mind among yourselves, which is yours in Christ Jesus, who, though he was in the form of God, did not count equality with God a thing to be grasped, but emptied himself, by taking the form of a servant, being born in the likeness of men.

PHILIPPIANS 2:5-7 (ESV)

3-D VISION

In the last days, God says, I will pour out my Spirit on all people. Your sons and daughters will prophesy, your young men will see visions, your old men will dream dreams. Even on my servants, both men and women, I will pour out my Spirit in those days and they will prophesy. I will show wonders in the heaven above and signs on the earth below, blood and fire and billows of smoke. The sun will be turned to darkness and the moon to blood before the coming of the great and glorious day of the Lord. And everyone who calls on the name of the Lord will be saved.

ACTS 2:17–21 (NIV); ALSO REFERENCE JOEL 2:28–32

When the servant of the man of God got up early the next morning and went outside, there were troops, horses, and chariots everywhere. "Oh, sir, what will we do now?" the young man cried to Elisha. "Don't be afraid!" Elisha told him. "For there are more on our side than on theirs!" Then Elisha prayed, "O Lord, open his eyes and let him see!" The Lord opened the young man's eyes, and when he looked up, he saw that the hillside around Elisha was filled with horses and chariots of fire.

2 KINGS 6:15–17 (NLT)

PILGRIMAGE

Blessed are those whose strength is in you, whose hearts are set on pilgrimage.

PSALM 84:5 (NIV)

SONG OF ASCENTS: PSALMS 120–134

In days to come the mountain of the Lord's house shall be established as the highest of the mountains, and shall be raised above the hills; all the nations shall stream to it. Many peoples shall come and say, "Come, let us go up to the mountain of the Lord, to the house of the God of Jacob; that he may teach us his ways and that we may walk in his paths."

ISAIAH 2:2–3 (NRSV)

TRINITY

Long ago God spoke to our ancestors in many and various ways by the prophets, but in these last days he has spoken to us by a

Son, whom he appointed heir of all things, through whom he also created the worlds. He is the reflection of God's glory and the exact imprint of God's very being, and he sustains all things by his powerful word.

HEBREWS 1:1–3 (NRSV)

For he will command his angels concerning you to guard you in all your ways.

PSALM 91:11 (ESV)

A great portent appeared in heaven: a woman clothed with the sun, with the moon under her feet, and on her head a crown of twelve stars. She was pregnant and was crying out in birth pangs, in the agony of giving birth. Then another portent appeared in heaven: a great red dragon, with seven heads and ten horns, and seven diadems on his heads. His tail swept down a third of the stars of heaven and threw them to the earth. Then the dragon stood before the woman who was about to bear a child, so that he might devour her child as soon as it was born. And she gave birth to a son, a male child, who is to rule all the nations with a rod of iron. But her child was snatched away and taken to God and to his throne; and the woman fled into the wilderness, where she has a place prepared by God, so that there she can be nourished for one thousand two hundred sixty days. And war broke out in heaven; Michael and his angels fought against the dragon. The dragon and his angels fought back, but they were defeated, and there was no longer any place for them in heaven. The great dragon was thrown down, that ancient serpent, who is called the Devil and Satan, the deceiver of the whole world—he was thrown down to the earth, and his angels were thrown down with him.

Then I heard a loud voice in heaven, proclaiming,

"Now have come the salvation and the power and the kingdom of our God and the authority of his Messiah, for the accuser of our comrades has been thrown down, who accuses them day and night before our God. But they have conquered him by the blood of the Lamb and by the word of their testimony, for they did not cling to life even in the face of death. Rejoice then, you heavens and those who dwell in them! But woe to the earth and the sea, for the devil has come down to you with great wrath, because he knows that his time is short!"

So when the dragon saw that he had been thrown down to the earth, he pursued the woman who had given birth to the male child. But the woman was given the two wings of the great eagle, so that she could fly from the serpent into the wilderness, to her place where she is nourished for a time, and times, and half a time. Then from his mouth the serpent poured water like a river after the woman, to sweep her away with the flood. But the earth came to the help of the woman; it opened its mouth and swallowed the river that the dragon had poured from his mouth.

REVELATION 12:1-16 (NRSV)

THE TABLE IS SET

Behold, I send an angel before you to guard you on the way and to bring you to the place that I have prepared. Pay careful attention to him and obey his voice; do not rebel against him, for he will not pardon your transgression, for my name is in him.

EXODUS 23:20–21 (ESV)

THE LORD'S PRAYER:

Pray then in this way: Our Father in heaven, hallowed be your name. Your kingdom come. Your will be done, on earth as it is in heaven. Give us this day our daily bread. And forgive us our debts, as we also have forgiven our debtors. And do not bring us to the time of trial, but rescue us from the evil one.

MATTHEW 6:9-13 (NRSV)

You prepare a table before me in the presence of my enemies; you anoint my head with oil; my cup overflows.

PSALM 23:5 (ESV)

You have heard that it was said "You shall love your neighbor and hate your enemy." But I say to you, Love your enemies and pray for those who persecute you, so that you may be sons of your Father who is in heaven. For he makes his sun rise on the evil and the good, and sends rain on the just and the unjust.

MATTHEW 5:43-45 (ESV)

Special Mention: Photo of Bible found in rubble of World Trade Center was taken by photographer Ira Block. http://www.ira block.com/Editorial/September-11/6

Rainbows and Roses

Don't let your hearts be troubled. Trust in God, and trust also in me. There is more than enough room in my Father's home. If this were not so, would I have told you that I am going to prepare a place for you? When everything is ready, I will come and get you, so that you will always be with me where I am.

JOHN 14:1–3 (NLT)

And this is the promise that he made to us—eternal life.

1 JOHN 2:25 (ESV)

God said to Noah, This is the sign of the covenant that I have established between me and all flesh that is on the earth.

GENESIS 9:17 (ESV)

Death and Life

And the dust returns to the ground it came from, and the spirit returns to God who gave it.

ECCLESIASTES 12:7 (NLT)

Jesus answered him, "Truly I tell you, today you will be with me in paradise."

LUKE 23:43 (NIV)

Truly, truly I say to you, you will weep and lament, but the world will rejoice. You will be sorrowful, but your sorrow will turn into joy. . . . So also you have sorrow now, but I will see you again, and your hearts will rejoice, and no one will take your joy from you.

JOHN 16:20, 22 (ESV)

WHEN WORLDS COLLIDE

Look! I am creating new heavens and a new earth, and no one will even think about the old ones anymore. Be glad; rejoice forever in my creation!

ISAIAH 65:17–18 (NLT)

So we fix our eyes not on what is seen, but on what is unseen, since what is seen is temporary, but what is unseen is eternal.

2 CORINTHIANS 4:18 (NIV)

In the beginning God created the heavens and the earth. The earth was formless and empty, and darkness covered the deep waters. And the Spirit of God was hovering over the surface of the waters. Then God said, "Let there be light," and there was light. And God saw that the light was good. Then he separated the light from the darkness. God called the light "day" and the darkness "night." And evening passed and morning came, marking the first day. Then God said, "Let there be a space between the waters, to separate the waters of the heavens from the waters of the earth." And that is what happened. God made this space to separate the waters of the earth from the waters of the heavens. God called the space "sky."

GENESIS 1:1-8 (NLT)

Another angel, who had a golden censer, came and stood at the altar. He was given much incense to offer, with the prayers of all God's people, on the golden altar in front of the throne. The smoke of the incense, together with the prayers of God's people, went up before God from the angel's hand.

REVELATION 8:3-4 (NIV)

Now when he heard that John had been arrested, he withdrew into Galilee. And leaving Nazareth he went and lived in Capernaum by the sea, in the territory of Zebulun and Naphtali, so that what was spoken by the prophet Isaiah might be fulfilled: "The land of Zebulun and the land of Naphtali, the way of the sea, beyond the Jordan, Galilee of the Gentiles— the people dwelling in darkness have seen a great light, and for those dwelling in the region and shadow of death, on them a light has dawned." From that time Jesus began to preach, saying, "Repent, for the kingdom of heaven is at hand."

MATTHEW 4:12-17 (ESV)

Then I saw a new heaven and a new earth, for the first heaven and the first earth had passed away, and the sea was no more. And I saw the Holy City, new Jerusalem, coming down out of heaven from God, prepared as a bride adorned for her husband. And I heard a loud voice from the throne saying, "Behold, the dwelling place of God is with man. He will dwell with them, and they will be his people, and God himself will be with them as their God."

REVELATION 21:1-3 (ESV)

THE LANGUAGE OF GOD

Suddenly, there was a sound from heaven like the roaring of a mighty windstorm, and it filled the house where they were sitting. Then, what looked like flames or tongues of fire appeared and settled on each of them. And everyone present was filled with the Holy Spirit and began speaking in other languages, as the Holy Spirit gave them this ability.

ACTS 2:2–4 (NLT)

For one who speaks in a tongue does not speak to men but to God; for no one understands him, but he utters mysteries in the Spirit.

1 CORINTHIANS 14:2 (ESV)

Likewise the Spirit helps us in our weakness; for we do not know how to pray as we ought, but that very Spirit intercedes with sighs too deep for words. And God, who searches the heart, knows what is in the mind of the Spirit, because the Spirit intercedes for the saints according to the will of God.

ROMANS 8:26–27 (NRSV)

Truly, truly, I say to you, whoever believes in me will also do the works that I do; and greater works than these will he do, because I am going to the Father.

JOHN 14:12 (ESV)

Garden Party

Awake, O north wind, and come, O south wind! Blow upon my garden that its fragrance may be wafted abroad. Let my beloved come to his garden, and eat its choicest fruits.

SONG OF SOLOMON 4:16 (NRSV)

And whatever you ask in prayer, you will receive, if you have faith.

MATTHEW 21:22 (ESV)

For as the earth brings forth its sprouts, and as a garden causes what is sown in it to sprout up, so the Lord God will cause righteousness and praise to sprout up before all the nations.

ISAIAH 61:11 (ESV)

GARDEN REFERENCES:

Garden of Eden, Genesis 2-4

Garden of Gethsemane, Matthew 26, Mark 14:32-52, Luke 22:39-46, John 18:1-11

Garden Tomb, John 19-20

Garden of the new Jerusalem, Revelation 22:3-5

Hymn: "In the Garden," C. Austin Miles, 1912, Hall-Mack Co.

EPILOGUE

It will be good for those servants whose master finds them ready, even if he comes in the middle of the night or toward daybreak . . . You also must be ready, because the Son of Man will come at an hour when you do not expect him.

LUKE 12:38, 40 (NIV)

About the Author

Thank you, dear reader, for visiting my garden. It is my prayer that, by engaging your heart, mind, and senses, you will have discovered that *you* are God's greatest delight. You can share your own story at our *Come to the Garden* website, www.come tothegardenbook.com, and even download group study materials for your book clubs and Bible study groups. And I've placed downloadable images of my watercolors painted especially for the book on our site. As I have invited you to share your stories, allow me to share a bit more about myself.

Raised in northeast Ohio on the shores of Lake Erie, I began cultivating my deepest passions at an early age, beginning with a close and loving family. Saturday morning lessons at the Cleveland Museum of Art fostered my great appreciation for fine art. An invitation as a young teenager to attend the Metropolitan

Opera's performance of *Madame Butterfly* as the guest of the opera's cellist inspired my love for music and theater. And our family's country home in southern Indiana nurtured the deep sense of peace I find in spending quiet time with God's creation.

And baseball! I grew up in Major League Baseball's Cleveland Indians organization, where my father served as physician and medical director. Attendance through the years at countless games and several World Series and Baseball Hall of Fame ceremonies carved a special place in my heart for America's favorite pastime.

I earned a bachelor of science degree in speech pathology and audiology from Kent State University and became a lifelong member of the Delta Gamma fraternity. In 1997, I relocated to Houston with my husband, Guy, and this is when I spent four inspiring years serving as a lay minister for the Spiritual Care Department at the Methodist Hospital.

Passionate about the study of God's Word, I am a seasoned Bible study and small group leader and an active member of The Woodlands United Methodist Church, where I also sing in the chancel choir.

On occasional weekends throughout the year, I can be found at area racetracks "pit-crewing" for my husband's auto racing weekends. My other interests include watercolor painting, cooking, gardening, reading, and spending time with our dogs.

Of all my passions, my greatest joy comes from the quiet devotional time I spend each morning. Spending time in prayer and praise "*establishes the foundation for my day. I take my Lord's hand and we approach each new day, each new adventure, together.*"